Geneva's Truth

A Prolific Story of Love, Loss, Forgiveness, and Truth

TOMEKA WALKER EWING

i

TABLE OF CONTENTS

Acknowledgements

I would like to express my heartfelt gratitude to the people who have made this book possible. I give praises and honor to the Lord for seeing me through some of my darkest days.

I honor my parents, John Earl Walker Sr. and Joan Walker, for providing me with love and never-ending support throughout my life. Thank you for believing in me, even when I didn't believe in myself.

I am forever grateful for my three children: Khadijah, Stanley, and Asia Ewing. You all keep me inspired to live. You encourage me to always be my best. To Stanley, my only son, living without you here on earth has been the hardest thing that I've ever had to do. But each time I stopped writing, I could hear your spirit speak to my soul, "Don't quit, Momma; you got this."

Special thanks to my sister Lucina Smalls. You are my angel here on earth. You keep me grounded, and I could not have finished my very first book without your love and support. And to my good friend Joshua Cerone, thanks for always speaking about life over this book and for reminding me daily of God's promise over my life. And to all my friends who encouraged me so often, there are too many to name, but you know who you are, and I love each one of you.

A special thank you to Mr. Aaron J. Mobley Jr. of AJM Unlimited for taking my manuscript and turning it into a beautiful masterpiece for the world to enjoy. Your expertise and direction on this project have been more than noteworthy.

1

The Foundation

Ve all have something that has occurred in our lives that we can never forget. That *one thing* that changed the dynamics of life can be the birth of a child, a new marriage, a job promotion, or a first kiss. But for some of us, that *one thing* is not so joyous, as it causes tears to form in your heart when you think about it.

I've had many joyous occasions, but that *one thing* that changed my life is not one of them. I've prayed many long prayers that this *one thing* would never have happened to me. I didn't think that I deserved such heartache. I didn't understand how the same God who loves us so much would also allow us to hurt so much. These were my thoughts before that *one thing* happened. I now see time in two ways, before and after that *one thing*. After that *one thing*, I grew to realize that every thought we think and every word that we speak are being manifested in our lives. From birth to death, we are our thoughts. We receive our heart's desires and our spoken words become the truth. After that *one thing*, I learned that the biblical scripture from Proverbs is so very true, "death and life are in the power of the tongue." Had I known this before that *one thing*, I would've spoken about life instead of death.

Life seemed perfect before that *one thing*. Yes, some would say that's not realistic, but it's true. There was a time before that *one thing* where I thought that I was invincible to pain and suffering. I lived in Harvard Square in Cambridge, Massachusetts, my older model Lexus was perfect, and its title was in my name. I'd bought it for cash at an auction, and it was perfect.

We lived in Harvard Square, and we had a large fenced-in backyard, with the most beautiful oak tree. I sat for hours and watched my three young children running around playing tag or kickball. Back then, it never dawned on me that having a yard that big was hardly heard of in Boston, nevertheless in Harvard Square. The city had little room for yards, and rather large buildings were popping up everywhere, but I still found solace just sitting there at that window.

The winters in Cambridge were especially beautiful. I'd never seen snow so thick or so white. I fell in love with the snow and loved to watch my children make snow angels or build snowmen. If I could create a time machine, I'd travel back to that time when my most precious memories with my children were created there.

We were a family that celebrated. I'd have a party for anything: the honor roll, birthdays, holidays, and promotions at work. And I was blessed with a group of friends who I enjoyed like family. Most of them were teachers at my children's school. I was sometimes called "the parent of the year" because I was so involved in their education. Their teachers would attend all our parties, and we'd play cards and laugh and talk long after the kids had gone to sleep. That was the way my parents had raised me. They were close to the people who were close to us, and when the party was over, the kids went to sleep so as not to disturb the adults enjoying their "adult time."

My kids had sometimes disagreed with the very close relationships that I had with their teachers and administrators. They said that it made it hard for them because they were expected to be "perfect." But in this life that I had created, they were perfect. My husband also did not agree with my relationship with their teachers, but after getting to know them, he accepted that they were really good people who had a lot in common with me. Besides, they adored my children and wanted the best for them.

My friends who were not teachers worked with me at the hospital, which was one of the largest in the Northeast. We did so many wonderful things together, and some of them said that they admired my perfect life. Little did they know it was just an illusion—a perception. But it was never my intention to fool anyone for I'd programmed my own mind into thinking that it was okay. Somehow it didn't matter how things were but how they appeared to be.

My husband had returned to school to get a second degree. I spent many long nights helping him with homework and studying. I enjoyed this time together because it was so authentic. I felt like I was always the brains of my small perfect family, but he was smart, too, and was a good provider.

I had been planning a big party to celebrate his latest degree. I invited all our friends and his family. I prepared the food myself. I wasn't a great cook, but when I took my time, it was usually pretty good.

That night was one of the best nights that we shared together. It was hard to surprise him, but I did my best to do everything while he was at work. My friends brought the drinks, and I bought a case of wine from my favorite whole foods store. I purchased some old-school R&B CDs that would cover as the DJ for the night. He loved old school Rap and R&B.

After he left for work, one of my closest friends came by to decorate the place, and when he returned that night, he was so surprised. It was important back then that everyone knew how proud I was of his accomplishments. The kids went downstairs to play while we celebrated and partied upstairs.

I invited my neighbors, who weren't my friends, but they were good neighbors. My neighbors to the right were physicians, the husband a neurosurgeon and the wife an obstetrician. I worked with physicians all my life, so we shared pretty good conversations, but I'd never been personal with any of the physicians at work.

However, the Kapoors were down to earth. This would be the first time that I'd invited them to any of our gatherings. Out of respect, I always told them when we were having a get together, so they would understand the surge of people coming and going. Our backyards were right next to each other and, though they were both fenced in, we could hear each other when we were outside.

They were from India and still celebrated all of India's holidays and, like us, the Kapoors loved to have gatherings. I could hear them on special occasions celebrating with their families and friends. I could smell the Indian food being prepared. Mrs. Kapoor had offered me a few of the dishes that she'd prepared on many occasions after we'd discussed how much my family and I enjoyed Indian food. She made the best gobi aloo, which is an Indian-style dish with cauliflower and potatoes. Her sweet chutney with potato bread was the absolute best. Our children played together often, and my son once dog-sat for them when they went away on vacation.

They joined us that night as we celebrated. We danced and laughed late into the night. For those few hours, I wasn't pretending. I was given an opportunity to be free, and I sipped wine and danced and made mixed drinks for my guests. My husband was pleased, and I knew that for that evening he was proud to have me as his wife. He was proud that his closest friends knew that he had a smart, sexy, and very fun wife. It wasn't hard to play the part on that night because I was truly happy in those moments. My friend Teresa kept everyone laughing at her silly jokes, and my children's teachers danced the night away. I was taken aback when on the way out, Mrs. Kapoor commented, "Thank you for inviting us. You guys are the perfect family." I quickly thought to myself, *I'd have to go back into my childhood to find a perfect time because this is not what it seems, Mrs. Kapoor.*

*****

In 1996, I moved to Boston from a very small town in rural South Carolina. Cloverville had a tightly knit population of about 450 people. We all knew each other, of course, in a town with one stoplight and one store. It was a place where we seldom heard of any crimes. We slept with our doors unlocked and windows open. We casually walked into a neighbor's house to borrow some flour without even knocking as we knew the door was open.

When someone died in our small town, we all gathered at the bereaved family's house for the week and made sure that they had hot meals each day and whatever else they needed. The town was filled with love. We greeted each other with love, so there was no doubt that we were loved here.

One of my fondest memories of my town was at our local festival. We called it the "Possum Trot," and thousands of people traveled to our town to share a weekend of love. I truly believe that so many people came to this festival because they felt the love in the town. We played games, saw live shows and a circus, and so much more.

We stayed out past dark until the Possum Trot closed. Then we walked home together while talking about the great time we had all evening. We felt so much pride that all the kids from the city had come to our hometown.

After the festivities, my parents always ended the night at a local dance hall. I loved to wait up for them and watch them come home all tipsy and entangled in each other. They would still be dancing to the music that only the two of them heard as they walked in the door. My dad always seemed to be in a daze when looking at my mom. She was beautiful, and she made our childhood beautiful.

Later in life, I always took pride in being a mother and wife. Growing up, I'd heard of women who struggled in their lives because they never had a father present, so they committed to the wrong man and didn't always make the best decisions when it came to men. Fortunately, I didn't have that problem while growing up as a young girl in the small town of Cloverville. My parents did a great job of giving me more love than my small heart could stand. My mom told me often that I was better than most people and things, and my dad made loving him so easy. He was big and strong, but still soft-spoken and gentle.

I remember the day that I fell in love with my dad. I was maybe five or six years old, and my mom was making dinner. My sister and I were sitting in the living room playing make-believe with our dolls. My dad was working late and darkness had started to darken the windows. I heard my mom mumbling to herself that he was late and that she didn't want his dinner to get cold.

Finally, the doorknob began to turn and my dad rushed in covered in a powdery dust that smelled like fresh-cut wood. The knees of his pants were worn, and his tool belt swung loosely from his waist.

As soon as he stepped through the door, he looked at my sister and me and said, "Sorry, y'all, I'm so late. We were trying to finish this job today so that we can get paid tomorrow."

An admiration and love that I'd never known could exist was formed on that day because I realized that my father was the man who would make sure that I did not have to suffer. On that evening, I fell in love with my dad all covered in sawdust, his dark skin reflecting the bright yellow dust, his short afro covered dusty as well. I fell in love with his willingness to work so hard to provide for us, and I watched him as he headed into the kitchen to kiss my mom. He loved this woman so much that when she got pregnant with me, he took her hand in marriage against the protests of her family. He made a vow to love, honor, and protect her.

It's been 40 years since that day, and each year I watch him fulfill his vow with such grace that I've lived my life searching for it. As I grew older, I admired the love that my parents shared. I admired the fact that they created a perfect family for my sister and me. We rarely saw them argue, and we often watched them kiss and cuddle sometimes as if they were the only two people on the planet. I wanted a perfect life just like the one that I had as a child, and I would get it, even if I had to invent it myself.

My mother did what many mothers fail to do during these times: she built my self-esteem. Every single day, she told my sister and me how important and beautiful we were. She also told us that we'd have to be tough to survive in this tough world. She emphasized that sometimes we'd have to fight, and she meant that literally.

When my baby sister was born, she didn't talk for a very long time, and when she did talk, her words came rushing out in a flutter. I wouldn't call it a stutter, but she didn't pronounce her syllables. No one but me understood what she was saying. My parents took her to a specialist who referred them to a speech therapist, and I wasn't sure how that would help, but my sister continued to live with her impaired speech. When she started the first grade, I was finishing up the third grade. It was our first time of being in the same hall together. My sister didn't talk much at school because she felt ashamed. She would, however, talk with me when I met her in front of her class.

One afternoon, I overheard a chubby kid calling my sister names. He mocked her and asked her if she was speaking Chinese. My sister started to cry, and this made me so angry. When we got home that afternoon, I told my mom about it.

She looked me straight in the eye and said, "You and your sister are one, so you have to protect her, and if anyone hurts her, then you have to make sure they don't do it again."

The next day, I went to school and saw my sister walking down the hall. I asked her a question that she could answer while Mr. chubby was standing right there. As soon as my sister answered, he started jumping in, "What are you saying, San Wa Tan?"

All of the other students in the hall started to laugh until I walked up to him and punched him smack dead in the mouth. I told him that if he ever made fun of my sister again, I would hurt him even more. I was tall and strong for my age—just like my father. It was at this moment that I learned not to turn the other cheek because after I stood up for my sister, neither the bully nor anyone else in the school ever mocked her again. Ironically, her speech began to improve after that incident.

If you know my sister Joanna today, you'd never know that she had speech difficulties when she was young, as she turned into the most talkative person in the world. Sure, I got into trouble for hitting that boy, but when I got home, my mom told me that she was proud of me.

She said, "Geneva, I'm not condoning the fact that you punched a kid in the mouth, but I'm proud that you stood up for your sister. You are the strongest one right now, and the strongest one is supposed to support the weaker one until they are stronger."

We prayed that night together as we always did, and mom told me to make sure that I asked God for forgiveness. "In order to love God, you have to love yourself because you are his perfect creation," my mom would always say. She told me that I was better than the other children. Does that sound harsh?

When I was much younger, I thought that it was, but as I grew older, I realized that she had raised me to be better than most people. No, she didn't condone fighting, but she did tell us that we'd have to fight to protect and defend ourselves. She had a higher standard of morals for me, and even when I drifted away from them, they were engraved in the essence of who I truly was. Was my childhood perfect? For me it was. I didn't have lots of money or luxuries, but I had more than enough love.

I now believe that everything I learned as a child formed the outline of my life. While my sister and I were growing up, my mother made sure that we understood one thing: "As a wife, you have to do whatever you have to do to keep your family together." I didn't totally understand that back then because things always seemed so together in my childhood. My mom later said, "Sometimes, you must close your eyes to things that don't bring value to your family and walk away from things to keep the peace."

I wish that I was half of the wife that my mom was to my dad, and maybe then I would've received half of the love and respect that she had received from my father. I thank my mom often for her sacrifice, for not ever showing my sister and I how hard life was, for sheltering us from the storms that I later learned had hit our home but didn't shatter anything. My mom created the perception of a "perfect life," but hers was not an illusion. My sister and I lived it with her.

I was also blessed with an older sister. Her mom and my dad had dated in high school just a few years before he met my mom. Latoya was three years older than me, and she was beautiful like my dad. Her dark skin and big dark eyes were alluring. Her hair and eyebrows were thick and jet black, making her look a little Native American.

When I was very young, I remembered my dad telling me that I had a big sister and that she lived in the next town over. He said that we'd go visit her soon. I must have been about three, and I was so excited. I wasn't sure why I hadn't met her before, but I was excited. I later learned that when Latoya was born, my dad was there and her mom had moved in with my father's mom for a short while, but they broke up shortly after that. The break-up wasn't bad, it just all happened. But my dad loved Latoya, and we loved our visits with her. On occasion, she would come with us and we'd take her to see our dad's mom, our Grandma Carrie who always commented on how much Latoya looked like my dad. She really did resemble him more than any of us. She even walked like him.

On our last visit, her mom informed my dad that they were moving to Atlanta. Georgia, and we wouldn't be able to see them often. She told my dad that she wasn't going to make him pay child support because she knew that he was struggling to make ends meet as it was and that she would provide for Latoya on her own. Here was my sister's mom, this single mom, thinking about the welfare of the man who'd fathered her only child. I'll never forget that day. It takes a lot of strength and courage to do such a thing. I would later admire the

9

petite mother of my sister. She was beautiful on the inside and out. And even though I didn't know it then, she was right: my father had barely made ends meet for us. We just never knew because he and my mother showered us with love. So, when mom said that we were eating light today because on Saturday we were going to have a feast for the family as we celebrated something, that's what we believed. We got excited to have our chicken noodle soup while anticipating Saturday. I later learned that my dad didn't get paid that week because the job had taken too long. Though he worked 12 hours some days, he got paid only after the job was completed, and sometimes they had to wait for an electrician to come before they completed the walls. I never knew this then, believing only that all things were perfect.

*****

Before that *one thing,* I didn't have any major mishaps in my life. Yes, I'd gotten pregnant in high school after planning a great future in college, but I found peace on August 22, 1995 when I looked into the eyes of my first-born daughter.

*****

In middle school and high school, I played any and every sport. My dad wanted a son, but my mom had me and my sister, so I was that son he never had. He spent quality time with me and taught me how to improve my jump-shot. One of the greatest memories I have as a child was playing ball with my father. I loved the gleam in his eyes when I made a shot. I started to believe that he was re-living his teenage years through me. He wanted me to do all the things that he couldn't do in life and so did my mom. My dad told me that he was forced to leave high school early to work and provide for his mother and younger brother. I never really understood how a 13-year-old would have to work and provide for a family, but it was my dad's character. No one physically made him work; instead, he made the decision to do so after a few nights of going to bed hungry. His mother had been a single parent and couldn't find suitable work in her small town. She also had other limitations. He loved his mother more than anything, so despite not being the oldest, he made a conscious decision to leave school and go to work. He was big for his age, so he said that it was easy for him to pose as an older boy and start working as a handyman for a construction company. He had

10

dreams of finishing high school and even going to college, but I watched him deposit his dreams in me. In my soul, I wanted to please my parents, as they deserved it after giving so much of their lives to providing for us.

I became pregnant during the winter break of 1994. We were having a holiday basketball tournament, and I was so sick to my stomach that I did not go. My dad was worried because I'd played basketball sick many times, and I had even tried to play with a torn ligament once, which caused me more pain than I could have imagined.

My mom was the first to become suspicious. She knew that I was sneaking around with this older boy from up north who had recently moved to South Carolina. The rumor around town was that he was a drug dealer in the city and was moving because of a threat on his life. That's one thing about small towns: rumors fly high. Truth is that he had moved to the south simply for a change. He had just completed junior college and wanted a break from city life. And I was sneaking around with him, and I was in love. So in love that it didn't matter that I was having unprotected sex because my mom had gotten pregnant with me this way and her life was perfect. When people talk about a generational curse, this is one aspect of it: the *mindset.*

Because we become every thought that we think, it was this kind of thinking that influenced my teenage pregnancy. I saw my mother being a wonderful teenage mom, and in my mind, I accepted that this was okay. I should've changed my thoughts to "My mom is the greatest, but I will not start a family until I am mentally and financially secure enough to provide the best possible life for this generation and the next." I do not believe that a generational curse is some black magic on a family's blood line. Instead, it is a chain of similar thinking that causes the same result to happen repeatedly. My maternal grandmother gave birth to her first child as a teenager and married my grandfather when they were both just 16 years old. My mom gave birth to me at 17 and I gave birth to my first daughter at 17. I'm sure that my mother's grandmother was a teenage mom, too.

I told my mom that I was not having sex with Gregory, my boyfriend, and I was not pregnant. In fact, I showed her that my monthly cycle was now on. I had to show her because she demanded that I do so a few weeks early by saying, "I'd better see a period or your little behind is grass." What my mom didn't know was that I had cut the bottom of my foot and put the blood on a maxi pad and placed it inside my panties. I'd done this out of pure desperation. I did not want to disappoint my parents, but I loved Gregory.

I did this for months, but my mom was nobody's fool. She said that something wasn't right and that she was taking me to the doctors the next day. I don't know why I tried to fool my mom for so long, as we all knew that she could predict anything from the weather to a winning lottery number. She predicted that I was pregnant, even though I displayed a monthly cycle and played basketball every single day.

I dreaded that doctor's visit, but I went anyway. Tests confirmed that I was four months pregnant at 17 years old. My father was devastated. It was only the second time that I'd ever seen that man cry, with the first being when we buried my grandmother. I watched tears fall from the eyes of the man who I had fallen in love with, and I wanted to bring him so much joy. Instead, I disappointed him, but like God, he forgave me quickly.

I told my older boyfriend Gregory that I was pregnant and that I wanted to be married and start a family. I wanted to give my daughter all the things that my mom and dad had given to me. My life changed that year. I walked down the aisle to get my high school diploma with a big belly and all hopes of my future gone. I also got married and started my perfect life. I was sad often as I watched my classmates start college, but I vowed to make this life as perfect as my parents' lives. After our marriage, we gave birth to a son. He was perfect. I thanked God on the night of his birth that he'd blessed me with a handsome baby boy. I named him James after his paternal grandfather. He became the love of my life.

*****

Life was not easy in South Carolina for a young family. The economy was not good at all, and the only jobs available to applicants without an education were factory jobs. I had promised myself that I would never work in a factory, but I had no choice. I went to a temp agency, and they placed me at a factory making batteries.

One day as I was standing on the factory line, I heard the words of my mom loud and clear, "You're better than this, Geneva." That evening, I went to the local technical college and registered for a medical administrative class. After nine months, I had completed the certification and headed to the local hospital as a radiology assistant. I became pregnant with our third child while working at that hospital. I didn't plan to have another child, but my mentality back then was simple, "I'm married and so I can have as many children as I want." We weren't financially ready for another child, but I did what my mother had done for us. I showered them with lots of love.

On the day that I went into labor with Ariel, I was at work. I should've been out on maternity leave, but we needed every dollar that we could get, so I worked up until the very minute before my water broke. It's funny now because when I felt the gush of warm fluid, my very first thought was, *I'm gonna miss a half-day's pay.* Ariel was beautiful, though, and the largest of our three children. She also had the most beautiful smile. After her birth, I said that she looked like my dad, and so she was surely my baby. A lot of crazy things were going on in South Carolina, and my husband made the decision to return to his hometown of Dorchester, Massachusetts.

I was nervous about moving to a big city, but I was also excited because I saw myself growing in a larger city. I've always had big dreams, with the biggest being having a perfect family, but also having wealth and independence from poverty. I didn't want my children to know anything about anything that didn't include happiness.

I'd learned that poverty was another generational curse that could be broken by simply doing the opposite of what had brought poverty to your family in the first place. I had a professor once who told a story about twin brothers who had grown up in a very abusive household. Their father was an alcoholic and abused their mother, and they all lived in complete poverty. Sometimes they lived in the dark and went to bed without food.

Their father had also been abusive to the twins. At 30 years old, one was an alcoholic sleeping on the streets. He had been in many relationships in which he was the abuser. The other twin had gone to medical school and was now a prominent physician and community activist with a wife and two children he adored. He volunteered in the inner city to help at-risk boys.

When the twins were asked, "How did your life turn out the way that it did, after you grew up in such poor living conditions?" Their answers were the same, "I didn't have any choice but to be who I am with an abusive alcoholic father." One twin used the reasoning to make the same bad decisions as his father, while the other used the same reasoning to make opposite decisions about his life.

Back in Dorchester, we moved in with his parents, and they were a blessing from God. They helped me with transportation and, most importantly, with my three children. My in-laws were financially stable and helped me with bills on so many occasions. They allowed us to live with them rent free for the first year, after which we paid. It was a great life for those two years. I worked two jobs so that we could afford to live in a nice neighborhood. I learned that there were some rough parts in Boston, and I didn't want to raise my kids in the inner city.

We were close to Roxbury. I'd heard about Roxbury because that's where an all-boy group, New Edition, was from, but it was a bad neighborhood. Drugs and gun violence were an everyday occurrence. Being from the rural south, I knew nothing about gangs, and my first experience would be my last. My son was playing on the porch with his friend Brian. We'd met Brian and his family as soon as we moved in. Kids always find kids with their same interests, and Brian loved sports. I went over to meet his parents because I didn't allow my kids to have friends whose parents I hadn't met. The mother was a single mom with two other children. She was from Cape Verde.

I'd never heard of Cape Verde. Where I was from there were only two kinds of people: African Americans and White Americans. She looked African American, but her accent was different. Her name was Claudette, and she was a beautiful person. Her parents had migrated to Boston in the 1970s during a time of total chaos in her country. She said that she'd planned on moving out into the suburbs to give Brian and his brother and sister a better life.

On a later day, James and Brian were playing on the front porch, and a few boys ran through the neighborhood followed by another group of young boys who each had guns and were all shooting at each other. I was at work, of course, but when I got home my son started explaining the events as if they were in a movie, "Momma, they were all shooting. The tall guy had a big gun like Rambo and his friend had a small shiny gun. We ducked under the porch, Momma, so we couldn't get shot, but they kept shooting." I cried that night. I wouldn't let my children learn anything else about this kind of life. I started to pack my things on that night because we'd save up enough money to move anywhere. We chose Cambridge because of its impeccable school system, great neighborhoods, and my husband would be closer to his work.

Moving from Dorchester to Cambridge wasn't the toughest task because we'd been staying with my husband's parents, and so the only things that we had to carry were our personal belongings. The children were excited to be moving because they would have their own rooms. My in-laws had been more than kind to allow us to stay with them for such a long time, but it was going to be nice to have our own space again. Our new house was small but spacious. Weird concept, but its spaciousness was in comparison to having lived in such tight quarters for such a long time. My son and two daughters shared bunk beds at our old place, but in our new place James had his own room.

Just a few years before that *one thing*, my oldest daughter had a close friend whose brother had been ill since birth. Doctors said Alex would only live to be two, but he and my son James still became close friends. Alex got sick during the summer that we moved into our beautiful place in Cambridge. It was scary, but he pulled through. I'd never really seen Alex sick, as he and James ran through the house as they headed to the basketball court where they played ball for hours. On the morning that I'd gotten the call that he was now admitted in the hospital and it wasn't good, my heart sank. I loved him like my own child, so I began to pray for him. I prayed to God to heal him. I believed that prayer changes things, but I've come to believe that nothing "not even prayer" can change the will of God.

Alex passed away, and it broke my heart. I didn't know how to face his mom; in fact, I didn't want to face his mom. I didn't want to go over to their house with my only son while she was without hers. On the night before the funeral, I prayed over my children's lives, and I told God that if anything were to happen to any of my kids, I would die. I told him that if I had to bury any of my kids, I would lose my mind.

I watched Alex's mom on the next afternoon in her black dress with her other children as the small coffin of her son was before them. I didn't want to meet her, and so I watched her and prayed that I would never become like her. I admired the fact that she could walk and that she said "thank you" as the people passed by to pay their respects. I loved her courage, but I cried all night. On that night, I went into my children's rooms as they slept, and I watched them. I wanted to stay there and watch them forever.

Before that *one thing*, I was just beginning to live out my dreams. I'd changed my outlook on life and was willing to do almost anything to be successful. But things changed drastically in the winter of 2010. That was a day that I believe laid the bricks that would serve as the foundation that would lead up to that *one thing*.

16

A good winter thus far with the kids just starting in their new charter school. They didn't want to leave the public-school system because they had so many friends and we were all family, but their father and I made the decision that they would be more successful academically in the smaller classrooms that the charter school offered.

My marriage seemed better before this winter. Yes, we had issues, sometimes more than I wished to acknowledge, but they seemed superficial to the love that we shared. I knew that my husband was unfaithful, and his unfaithfulness didn't shake me. At this time, it was more important that my marriage resembled that of my parents. There had been many affairs between the two of us. My mom once said that early on she and my dad had struggled to keep the marriage afloat, but one thing she always told me was "a woman can't do the things a man does." I heard my mom loud and clear, but I didn't listen. Around the tenth time that I found out my husband was unfaithful, I thought, *If it's good for the goose, it's good for the gander.* Therefore, we had affairs, and I prayed that he was always using protection as I had always done with other lovers, and I didn't feel any remorse for my actions.

Life appeared perfect because my husband and I both worked good jobs. We lived in one of the most affluent neighborhoods in the country, our children were tall and beautiful, and we were both very attractive. We woke up each morning and both ran a few miles. He'd come back in time to walk the kids to school. To the naked eye, my life was perfect.

There were times when we each found out about the other's lover, and we argued about it for a little while. I made myself believe that if we were respectful of each other, we could keep this marriage forever. There was only one stipulation, and I was very clear with him about it: I would not accept a child out of wedlock. That was the only reason that I'd leave this seemingly perfect marriage. I mean if we're both using protection with other lovers, this should never become a problem, so our perfect life could continue until the end of time.

You see, in my mind at that time, having a child outside of the marriage would be too complicated because we'd have to allow not only the child but also the mother into our perfect lives. I knew this marriage couldn't take an openly acknowledged confession of our infidelity. Our relationships would only be known to the two of us. Our children, our parents, and our friends were never to know, and they were only allowed to know what we displayed.

It takes a lot of strength to admit to being a part of a traumatic event. Usually when bad things happen, the reason is usually someone else's fault because we wouldn't hurt ourselves. That's what I used to think, but everything that happens to us, whether good or bad, is a direct cause from ourselves. It took me some time to get to this revelation, and I've since taken full responsibility for all of the things that have happened in my life, including that *one thing*.

2

Pleasure and Pain

I knew he was now seeing someone at work. I had smelled her Bath and Body Works products on him on a few occasions, which was fine because I'd recently met a very young and handsome Jamaican gentleman on my part-time job. He asked if I was married because I always wore my wedding band unlike my husband who never did. He said it was because he worked with his hands. I remembered my dad always wore his wedding band, even though he did construction and his hands would be all bruised sometimes, but his wedding band always illuminated his strong dark left hand. I told Daniel that I was married, but, of course, not happily. In his strong Jamaican accent, he replied, "Oh my, that's not good." We flirted for a few months, while I assumed my husband continued to see his newest lover. Right before Thanksgiving, my husband said that he was going on a weekend trip to the casino with one of his childhood friends. I thought to myself, *This thing must be serious if he's going all weekend.*

One thing that we'd always done was be respectful. He asked me if I was okay with it, so I called Daniel to see if he was free for the weekend and if he wanted to meet. I told my husband that his plan was perfectly fine, and then I called my mother-in-law Shirley to babysit for the weekend. I was blessed to have the most wonderful in-laws. They didn't pry or ask questions, and I always felt like they knew their son was unfaithful me and probably that I was also unfaithful. I talked to my mom that week, and I told her that Gregory was going away for the weekend. She got quiet on the other end of the phone for a few moments and then she replied, "It's never a good idea for your husband to be spending the night out away from home, Geneva. Remember you have to do what you have to do to make your marriage work."

I wanted to tell my mom, "That's what I've been doing. All these years, I've been doing what I must do. I've been ignoring the smell of other women on my husband. I've been ignoring the bathroom conversations. I've been ignoring the lack of sexual attention and attraction to me. I've been doing all of that, and I've been indulging in my own affairs." I wanted to confess to her right then and there. I wanted to cry, but this was my perfect life.

I told my mom that it was perfectly okay with me, and Gregory worked very hard and deserved this weekend trip. I lied to my mom by telling her that he'd invited me, but I had a weekend conference at work, so I suggested that he take his close friend. The lies we tell are sometimes just for perception.

Daniel and I met in downtown Boston at a very upscale restaurant for dinner. I reserved a hotel room for the weekend and included a day of spa and relaxation. I was 12 years his senior and being with him took me back to my younger days. Over dinner, he told me how much he admired my beauty, and when he first met me, he thought that I was 23 or 24. He worked out a lot, so his muscles made him appear older. He talked about his dreams of becoming a doctor here in the United States. He talked about how hard life was in Jamaica, and he reminded me again of my dad. He was working two jobs to provide for his family with the hopes of starting medical school soon. He was strong and gentle. He was perfect for me in that moment.

The next day, we awoke from what I would call one of the best nights of my life, and we headed out to the Charles River to run a few miles. We stopped in at a small coffee shop near the North End, and we talked about our childhoods. We had so much in common. His parents didn't have much money, but they had showered him with love. They lived on a farm in rural Kingston, Jamaica, and his dad worked hard with his hands. His sisters and brothers were all younger than my youngest child. I didn't talk about my husband or my children at all. When he asked about them, I just told him that the marriage was over.

We returned to the hotel after coffee and prepared for our afternoon massages. Daniel kept watching me as I got dressed. His eyes seem to be taking my clothes back off, one garment at a time. I can't remember the last time my husband had marveled at my beauty. I was a beautiful woman. My mom had given me this confidence and so did the mirror. I'd never worn makeup because I never had to. My skin was a rich tone of brown, and the only blemish was my birthmark, a mole to the right of my nose. And there were no stretch marks or blemishes on my body either. I thanked God for making me so perfect. I wondered if my husband would find a woman with such beauty, especially one who gave birth to three kids in five years.

When we were leaving the hotel for the lobby, Daniel stopped in the doorway. I almost tripped over him because we were running late for our one o'clock massages. In his thick sulky Jamaican accent, he whispered into my ear, "I'm so jealous of your clothes because they get to touch your body all day." He took my breath away. Was he really this smitten over me?

When we reached the massage parlor downstairs, I requested a female masseuse and she was beautiful. She was young and probably Italian with her smooth olive skin and long black hair. She was mysteriously beautiful. One thing that I loved about being with Daniel was that unlike my husband, he never looked at other women when I was with him. My husband would watch any half-decent-looking woman who walked by, but Daniel didn't take his eyes off me while this beautiful young woman was giving him an amazing massage. He blew me kisses and I caught them. I was thankful for this day, as I needed to be with a man who only saw me and my greatness from time to time.

After our massages, we headed for dinner at a very quaint restaurant on Beacon Street. I had been a vegetarian for many years now, so I ordered the eggplant parmesan. Daniel commented that he could never join me in the vegetarian world because he loved meat too much. He admired my dedication to giving up meat as a lifestyle.

My health was very important to me. When I moved to Boston years before, I was very overweight. I didn't realize how much because I was tall, and I didn't accumulate any fat along my stomach. My first visit to the doctor here is when I realized there was an issue. The doctor went over the BMI chart with me and explained that I was "obese." I'd never thought in a million years that my five-foot, seven-inch frame at 190 pounds was obese, but the doctor had spoken with such urgency that he scared me.

I started running and eating lean and lost 30 to 40 pounds within the next six months. I decided to give up meat after watching a documentary on the discovery channel one evening with my kids that showed how meat is processed in America. I felt bad for the animals, so my children and husband and I gave up meat.

Of course, I didn't tell Daniel the full story because I didn't feel it was fair to talk about my kids around him. He was my separate life, and I could never mix him with my perfect life. He was my getaway from the pressures of being perfect. I could let my hair down and just enjoy life. I didn't have to pretend. When I think back now, it's weird how free I was that weekend. Here I was a "happily married" woman parading around the city like a single teenager. I prayed that night that whoever "she" was that my husband was spending the weekend with was bringing him as much satisfaction as Daniel had brought to me. He'd awaken that young girl in me, the one who had dreamed to be all these great things one day. When our weekend together was over, I felt revived, and I started to investigate enrolling back into college to pursue my master's degree.

At home, my husband and I returned nicely back into our perfect lives. It's funny because I never asked him about his trip to the casino with his friend, and he never asked me about my weekend without the kids. Most people, even friends, would ask, "Did you win any money?" He knew that the kids were with his mom, and so we never talked about the weekend. That was perfect. I learned very early that if I really wanted a marriage like my parents, then dealing with what I had meant learning not to ask questions. Besides if the goose was doing the same things as the gander, then it all washed out. And I didn't want to stop seeing Daniel; in fact, I wanted to see him more.

He wasn't my first affair, just the one that brought value into my life. We spent every lunch break together just talking. Over lunch one day, he said, "Geneva, I have been praying about my feelings for you, and they are wrong. You are still married, and being with you is against God's law." All my life I relied on God only when I needed him and, in this perfect life, I didn't need him for anything right now. What I needed was to convince this young man that being with me was not the end of the world. I told him what I had not told anyone, "My husband and I are getting divorced soon, so if you can just wait a while...." I told him how unfaithful my husband had been all our lives, and that he was the only man that I'd ever cheated with. He said he didn't understand how a man could be unfaithful to a woman like me. He said that I was perfect, so we continued to see each other. I didn't feel guilty at the time for lying about my marriage being over. The truth was I didn't want my marriage to be over. I didn't want the perfect illusion that I had created to end. Daniel and I took long walks after work, we talked for hours on the phone, we laughed together, and we began to pray together. During this time with Daniel I forgot that my husband was probably forging the same kind of relationship with whoever "she" was.

You see of all the affairs that my husband and I had shared, none of them took up too much of our time. I mean if I was talking to Daniel for three to four hours a day, why hadn't my husband noticed. And what was he doing during these times? I had no idea; I was only concerned with getting out of the house to spend quality time with the young man who was sparking flames that I had forgotten ever existed.

One night, Daniel and I were praying together, and he prayed that my divorce would be expedient. For the first time, he told me that he was in love with me. This is not what I signed up for as I only wanted a good time. I wanted the attention and affection of a new lover. I wanted late night rendezvous and hot and steamy quick nights. I started to feel convinced to end the relationship. It was never my intention to have him fall in love, but I had seen it coming. The way he looked at me had changed from lust to compassion. I tried to talk to him that night about "slowing things down," but he was already there, and I was far behind with my perfect life. Therefore, I had to end this relationship soon. As for my husband, I hoped that he would not allow anything like this to happen to him. We had to keep the affairs from interrupting our perfect lives.

I told Daniel on that night that I had not been completely honest with him. I told him that I did not file for divorce and was still with my husband. He cried and I cried. I started to look for another part-time job because I needed to get away from him. He was perfect. I found a new job and I changed my phone number. He emailed me from time to time, but it was left there.

When I didn't have an affair to run to, I felt jealous, so I had to look for a new affair, which for me wasn't hard at all. I was 34 years old with a flat stomach and hips that looked as though they were sculptured onto my body. Many people didn't believe that I had birthed three kids who were now teenagers. My smile was sweet and kind as my heart. My brown skin was so radiant that if you walked into a crowded cafe of people of different nationalities, you'd ask yourself who I was in the crowd. My mom said that I was "easy on the eyes." I have to agree with her and thanked her for such good genes. Still, I had standards when choosing a lover. For example, I needed him to resemble my father: big and strong. I needed him to be loving, kind, humble, and hardworking. He had to love his mother and he had to adore me.

I didn't find a replacement lover for Daniel, so I continued to focus on myself and the kids. My son had started a new baseball team and was playing on an AAU basketball team. I was busy traveling with him. On some of those days, my husband would stay out of the house. I assumed he and his lover were getting some quality time, but when there was a big game or event, we all jumped in my Lexus and drove there as one big happy family.

I always thought that I had the advantage over my husband's other lovers because I was the mother of his three children. If I wanted to impede on some of his time, all I had to do was create some family event, as I knew he would have to call off his plans. My son's team made it to the city championships in baseball that year, so I took my husband away from his lover every weekend in October; besides, I didn't have a lover at that time. It was kind of nice to make plans for my family every weekend. It reminded me of the days before the drift, the days before I met Daniel, and the days before my husband met his newest lover who seemed to be taking up so much of his time.

*****

Looking back to that winter evening in 2010, it was so dark and snowy, though it was only around six o'clock. My husband had taken our son for a haircut, rushing out to get there on time because he came home late from work. I started dinner and began to study when I thought I heard my phone ringing, but it wasn't mine. It was my husband's phone. I decided to answer it. If he was anything like me, then he would have already told his lovers that he couldn't answer the phone during certain hours.

When I picked up the phone, a woman asked for my husband. I expected her to hang up after hearing my voice, but she was anxious to speak to him and sounded very young. I told her that I was his wife, and I asked if she wanted to leave a message for him because he was at the barber shop with our son.

She burst into her story about being Alicia, being his girlfriend, and being pregnant and now starting a family after my husband told her that he was divorcing me and marrying her. For a split second, I wanted to die; better yet, I wanted to kill him. I was sure that he was smarter than this. I mean he'd been having affairs on me since 1995, but he knew the rule: no disrespect or children out of wedlock.

I ended my marriage on that day. I told Alicia that she could come to my house and get his things. They would be packed and on the sidewalk in an hour. I was in such good shape that I gathered all the trash bags that I had in the kitchen and began to pack them. I emptied his closets and dressers in less than an hour.

Yes, I ended my marriage on that night. I packed all his things and sent him on his way. He didn't give me much push-back. He denied the pregnancy, but my spirit knew that it was true. I wanted to run and hide because I didn't want anyone to see my perfect life fall apart. I wanted everything to go back to normal, and I didn't want to take any responsibility for these events. It was solely his fault and hers. When I said that my mom gave me more than enough strength to survive in this life, I really meant it. My mom taught me how to pray and seek God. Some people believe that you must go to a church and that you must call upon the elders of the church, but my mom didn't believe that. Instead, she believed that we could call on the Lord our God at any hour of the day or night, no matter what our situation was, and he would come and see about us. I called on the Lord for help because I didn't know how I was going to make it.

One thing that came to my mind was if the baby was not born, I could take my husband back and return to our perfect life. I called my husband and asked him to meet me in Harvard Square so that we could talk. We met at the Starbucks on the corner, and I pleaded with him to talk to this young girl and ask her to abort the child. I had researched all her information and so I knew exactly who she was. She was just four years older than my daughter, and she was just a kid who probably got caught up in the charm of my older, handsome husband. He continued to deny the pregnancy, but I also knew she was pregnant according to a friend who worked at the hospital in Malden where she lived. On that evening, I prayed that the child would die. Yes, I did something so evil. I needed my perfect life back. If the child died, then we could move on like nothing had ever happened.

I started to search for God and then realized that my heart was too far from him. My heart was too far from my mother and father. I was too ashamed to call and talk to them about this *thing*. I used to talk to my parents about anything. I talked to my mom once about my own desire to be unfaithful and that it was my husband's fault. She reminded me that I was not a man and could not do manly things. She reminded me that my body was sacred and to lay with any man other than my husband was against God. I knew this, but it was not the way things worked for us. Our old way made us perfect. But I could not tell my mom about this *thing*—his unborn child—or that I'd put my husband out. She lived 1,000 miles away and would never know…right?

Instead, I continued to seek God. I started going to a church very close to my home. My children and I went faithfully, but I didn't find God there. What I did find were a whole lot of rules and regulations, preached sermons, title seekers, money junkies, and people claiming to be saved but who couldn't say hello. I found everything there but God, so I continued to seek God for myself. I studied the word of God, prayed for forgiveness, and fasted.

I heard God say with authority that my words were powerful. I started to study the power of these words. I studied affirmations from a biblical and non-biblical standpoint, and what I came to realize was that all the words that I'd spoken were valid and had the ability to come to pass. They did. I went to the library and visited the self-help section. My first book of affirmations was written by an older woman, Louise Hay. She wasn't religious at all just very spiritual. I had tried religion, and it didn't seem to work for me. What religion didn't do for me during that time was build me up. Instead, it made me think that I wasn't any more than a sinner. It went against all that my mom had told me. *I was surely more than that.*

With all the new craziness going on in my perfect life, I had to find help soon. What I didn't realize then, I found in the scriptures later in the Book of Luke 10: 19, "Behold, I have given you authority to tread on serpents and scorpions, and over all the power of the enemy, and nothing shall hurt you." Initially I couldn't believe that I had that much power, so I began to search for it. I needed to dig deep, and I needed to do it without limitations.

Everything in my beautiful house was a reminder of the perfect life that I no longer had. I wanted to move away from the beautiful city that I loved because I didn't want to run into my husband and his new young girlfriend. I heard from people around town that they had seen them here and there because Cambridge is a very small town. I didn't tell people that I was separated and had filed for divorce, yet they looked at me pitifully while thinking that my husband was cheating on me. What they didn't know is that he'd always cheated on me. Our life had been nothing more than the infidelity on which it was grounded. We just looked so perfect.

I found an apartment outside of the city and close enough to the children's new charter school that they could walk. But I was so depressed. I continued to seek the power within me because I had been depleted of all my strength. Things were difficult for the kids, too, and I wished that I had taken more time to help them, but I had been so self-absorbed in my own pain that I didn't realize they were hurting, too. I was angry because, for the first time in a long time, my husband had a lover, and I didn't. I was angry because very soon the world would see my perfect life come to a perfect end. I decided to seek out professional help. I had never heard of anyone in my family seeking professional help for depression, but as I prayed, I realized that I needed something else.

My son was the first to display feelings of hurt. He didn't see his dad anymore, and I had been too embarrassed to tell them that their dad had another child. I now know that my children weren't dumb; in fact, they were very smart and had figured some things out on their own. I decided to have family therapy sessions. It must have been hard for the kids to see their perfect lives crumple before them. One thing that we'd always done was make sure that the kids did not suffer in our wrongdoings. We had kept them safe, but now they were unsafe. They were now left with a single mom who had been strong and powerful but who was now depressed and confused.

My son didn't like the therapy and refused to talk at all to the therapist. I cried during each session. The therapist was a very short and plump older woman with blond hair. She was also divorced and knew the impact on the children. She said that it was important that I tried to keep things as normal as possible for the kids. I tried to take her advice, but it was difficult. The kids missed their dad, and though he provided for them financially, he was physically and emotionally unavailable. I must also admit that I was emotionally unavailable for them, too. I was so caught up in the fact that my perfect life was over and the man who I'd played house with for years was now living in a small apartment across town with his teenage lover and her mother. I was once a young lover some 20 years ago. Were they going to get married? Would she have my perfect life?

I had to do my best and get back into the swing of life. I couldn't just give up. I had to move on with my new life. I continued to study and put all my energy in myself and my children. The girls seemed to be doing well and had close friends. Most of these friends didn't have fathers around so it was normal to them. They were now a part of the normal family structure of most of the kids they knew. But James started to pick up a new set of friends. I didn't approve of them because I didn't know their families. They were from the inner city, and he was starting to catch the bus into the city to hang out with them. I asked him where he'd met them, he told me from AAU basketball. I didn't have a good feeling about them. He broke curfew repeatedly and developed an attitude like, "You can't tell me what to do. Where's my dad?" It broke my heart because he was my heart.

Having a son was one of the biggest blessings of my life. I adored him and made a vow to God that he would not be a statistic and that he would become the first doctor in our family. He was smart and charming and handsome. If you met him, you wanted to be around him. He had influence in the community and in school, and his image was important. I believed that was one of the reasons he had taken the separation and divorce from his dad the hardest. He loved his dad and wanted to be just like him, so it was important to me that he didn't know how his father really was. I tried to hide it as much as I could. I didn't want him to know how I really was either. But we needed to talk, so I asked him if he'd like to go to dinner with me to one of his favorite Chinese restaurants. He agreed and we headed out the door. It was cool, and as we got into the car, I grabbed his hand. He held my hand, and I told him how much I loved him. I loved holding his hand, which he no longer allowed me to do in public. When we were alone, I would always reach for his hand.

Dinner was great, and as we were heading home, my gas light came on. I hated pumping gas, so I thought it was perfect that my son was in the car. He'd pump my gas. I pulled up to the gas pump and said, "I'll go inside and pay and you pump, Son."

As I headed back to the car, a small dark sedan pulled up to the gas pump next to me. In the passenger seat was my estranged husband. I looked at the back seat and there was his new baby. I wanted to run because I didn't want my son to see this. I wanted to run up to my husband and slap him. We had a perfect life. I allowed him to be with other women, and all he had to do was keep himself and his family protected.

I walked over to the car and never looked at the teenage girl behind the wheel. I blamed him, not her, for destroying our family. He looked confused but unapologetic.

He asked me, "Why are you in my face? Aren't we separated?"

"Yes, we're separate because you had another child while you were married to me."

I called him every name I could think of, and the young girl jumped out of the car ready to fight.

She said, "Don't be talking to my man like that in front of my baby."

I wanted to slap some sense into her, too.

"Do you really think he's going to stay with you? You were with him while he was 'happily married' to me."

I wanted to choke the life out of her and take my husband back home so we could continue with our perfect lives. But I forgot that my son was standing right across from us pumping my gas. I looked over at him, and I saw a look of disappointment and pain. I wanted to run over to him and hold him, but I was too upset with his dad. He asked me if that was his dad's new girlfriend, and I didn't answer. I didn't think he saw the baby in the car because he didn't mention it. My husband and I had tried not to tell them about the baby. It was crazy to think that they wouldn't find out, but we thought that it was best.

An amazing evening out with my son had turned into craziness. All because his dad had violated our non-verbal agreement. He had done the *one thing* that destroyed our perfect life.

My son and I rode back home in total silence. We never spoke about that night again, and if he saw the child, he never mentioned it. After I got home, I cried myself to sleep. I listened to all the voices talking in my head: *you're not good enough; you're too old; you're not sexy enough; your life was a lie; he's never really wanted you; your perfect life was a joke.* I wanted to die that night, but I did that awful *thing* again: I wished that the baby would just die, so that I could have my perfect life back.

My son was different after that night. He was more reserved from me and seemed less interested in the family. He continued to hang out with his new friends, and I continued to worry about him. I'd already filed for divorce, but I decided that I would continue to sleep with my estranged husband. Not because I wanted him back, but because I wanted his new girlfriend to see how it felt to be cheated on. I called him over when the kids weren't there and kept him late. I loved to hear his phone ring and watch him ignore it. Let her sit at home and cry over my husband. I got satisfaction not from the sex but from the devious act of cheating with my own husband. I asked him once if he loved her and he denied it. I hoped that he did love her. I'd never lose my family over anything other than love. I continued to rendezvous with my husband until the divorce was finalized.

On the day that the divorce was final, I called him over while the kids were in school, and we spent the evening together. We laid there and thought about our old life. He said that he thought we could make it work. Silly thought because I'd never accept a child out of wedlock. That had been the *one thing* that couldn't be forgiven. He'd crossed the line of no return, and now he was little more than a payback to me.

I continued with him in this way for months. I never let the kids know that I was sleeping with their dad. I didn't want my daughters to think that I was such a fool. But I wanted his new little girlfriend to sense that he was with me. Women can always sense when their man is with someone else. Maybe she was too young to have that women's intuition yet, but I took as much of his time away from her and that new child as I possibly could. I was usually numb laying there with him, feeling only pain.

I couldn't continue like this, and so I started to read my self-help books again. It didn't make sense that for the entire year after my divorce, I was still sleeping with my ex-husband for revenge on his new lover. I was keeping myself in a toxic space, and if I didn't move out of that space soon, it would kill me. I continued to push my way through, and I decided that it was time for me to heal my life. I needed to make sure that my children didn't pick up any of these negative habits that their father and I had indulged in for most of their lives. Yes, we looked like perfect parents. We provided materialistically, but we were living a lie. I began to pray for forgiveness from God because twice in the last year I had wished death upon the life of a child. My mother would be so disappointed if she knew I had done such a thing—twice. My father would turn away in shame, and my children would not even believe that those words left my mouth.

I called my dad a few weeks later, and I talked to him about the things that were happening in my life. I didn't tell him about my now ex-husband's baby, but I told him about the divorce. I told my mom, and she cried. I told them that I was worried about my son and the time he was spending in the inner city. I told my mom that I thought that I might lose my mind one day. I heard voices, and they were always degrading me. I was seeking psychiatric help, but I also believe in my heart that I possessed the power to heal myself. My dad asked if my ex-husband was available to help with our son and I told him that he was not. He barely saw the kids, and we lived in the same town. My dad suggested that I send James down south where things were slower, and he would help to raise him up into the young man that I always hoped he would be. I talked to my son about it, and he didn't take it too well at first. He felt as if I didn't want to be with him because I wasn't with his dad. I explained to him that I wanted only the best for him and so did my dad. His sisters and I would also be moving soon, as I needed to get as far away from Boston as I could so that I didn't have that constant reminder of being hurt.

After the school year ended, I sent my son on a flight to South Carolina to live with my parents. He would be sleeping in my old bedroom, and he would receive the love that I'd received as a kid. My mom and dad would make sure that he was loved and happy. I couldn't give him that at the time. The girls weren't excited about having their brother leave. I explained to them that we would be moving down there soon.

When I think back now, I wish that his dad had stepped in and said, "I'll raise my only son. I'll help you with him," but he was caught up in the idea of having a teenage girlfriend and a new baby. I had similar feelings during my weekend with my young lover Daniel. That feeling takes you back in time and you feel young, free, and invincible again.

Without having to worry about my son getting into trouble in Boston, I began to continue to seek the God within me. I'd done some not so godly things, and I needed to be renewed. I started running and spending my evenings in prayer by the Charles River. I'd stay at the river for hours just praying. It is true that prayer changes things because the more I prayed, the more my life improved. I had to begin the process of forgiving everyone for everything. I had to forgive myself, and I had to forgive God. Yes, I blamed God for allowing my perfect life to be turned upside down. I forgave God, and I started to ask him for forgiveness. I needed God to forgive me for my sins and for the words that I had spoken in my anger.

I didn't go to church during this time. I didn't need rules, regulations, or boundaries. I just needed God in honesty, in pureness, and in line with his perfect will. I needed to hear his voice. I didn't see or sleep with my ex-husband during this time. I needed to purify my mind, body, spirit, and soul. It was a process, and I did it alone. I spent months by the Charles River, where I'd run for a few hours and pray for a few hours. For some reason, I could not seem to forgive my ex-husband. I was so hypocritical back then. I mean, I'd indulged in the same type of infidelity that he had. I'd taken other lovers while I was a married woman, but I blamed him for taking it too far. He allowed it to break up our family, and I thought that he shouldn't be forgiven.

3

The Transition

One evening as I sat in prayer, I heard the voice of God saying that he heard my command of death upon my husband's new child. He'd heard all my commands. When I told the lie that I was in the process of a divorce, it was his will that it would come to pass. I became scared and nervous. I had not meant it; I was only angry. It was confirmed on this day by the voice of God that words have power. What you say can and will manifest in your life. You have the power to speak life and death. I'd spoken death, and God had heard me. I started to run and ran for hours that night. I ended up running to my ex-husband and his new girlfriend's apartment. I stood outside and cried and begged God to please forgive me for saying such an awful thing. I made a vow to never speak of death again.

I walked back home, and it seemed like I was walking for hours. I knew that God was a forgiving God, but I also realized the weight of my words. When I got back home, my daughters were up and said they were worried about me. I'd been gone for more than eight hours without my cellphone. I told them that I was sorry and that I loved them more than anything in the world. I also told them I was getting better each day so that one day I'd be back to normal.

I called my mother's house to speak to my son. My mom said that he'd had a good week. He'd started basketball practice, and he and my dad were spending lots of time together going fishing and doing other father/son things. I told him that I loved him, and I asked for his forgiveness. I told him that I'd be moving back there soon, and we'd be a family again.

I started planning our return to South Carolina. I needed to be back with my new family—not my perfect family. I needed to be with my daughters and my son in a healthy real relationship. The days of pretending and living a lie were over. I loved the city of Boston, but it was not my home. The city had been good to me. I'd met some of the most amazing diverse people. I met people that I now consider family. One of my closest friends, Grisel, is a vibrant, speak-your-mind Puerto Rican who is just as close to me as my own sister. She taught me to be free-spirited and not take everything so seriously. She was the first person that I told the truth to about my past perfect life. Grisel and I met at work and instantly became close friends. I learned very quickly that I didn't have to pretend to be anything with her. She allowed me to be myself without judgement.

The second time that she commented on how perfect my life was, I interjected with "Gregory and I appear happy, but we're not. I've been with a man who's never been faithful to me not one day of our lives, and the truth be told, I've been just as unfaithful to him. We stay together because we are respectful, we keep our affairs hidden beneath layers of stones, and we dare not let anyone turn over one of those precious stones."

Grisel waited a few minutes before she spoke. When she did in her thick Spanish accent, she said, "Hey, Chicka, if it works for you all, why not?" She was the first person to whom I confessed my sins. I didn't confess them to God, as back then I thought, *God knows my heart, he knows that I'd prefer to be in an honest relationship, he knows that I'd for once like to be faithful to one man and have him be faithful to me.*

Another of my closest friends was Teresa, a beautiful blonde Irish queen who always kept me smiling with her genuine love and kind spirit. Teresa and I also met at work and became instant friends. After my marriage ended, I spent holidays with Teresa and her big Irish family. She had 10 siblings, and her mother was one of the sweetest women that I'd ever met. I'm not talking about nice or pleasant, but about a spirit so sweet that she could change the atmosphere in a room by simply walking into it. When Teresa and I first met, she had just lost her dad to cancer. He was a patient at the hospital where we worked, and I loved the way their family rallied together through those difficult times. The love that they displayed reminded me so much of my own family. It's one of the reasons why of all the places I could've spent Christmas or Thanksgiving, I chose to go to Teresa's. Her family reminded me of my own family, which wasn't as large but was still perfect.

Teresa had a group of friends who were some of the most outgoing and dynamic people that I've ever met. One summer she invited me for a weekend getaway to Cape Cod. The Cape Cod region includes Martha's Vineyard and Nantucket and has the most beautiful beaches with rolling dunes. We left Boston on Friday evening after work.

This was one of my first weekend trips away from home. I wasn't meeting anyone, and when I asked Gregory if he minded me going away with the girls for the weekend, he had a gleam in his eyes that answered before he said, "No problem. Sure."

When we got to the rental house on the ocean, Teresa's friends were already there and partying. One thing I loved about her friends was that they were strong hardworking women and they played just as hard. I had so many drinks on that night, I couldn't think. I really didn't want to think because I knew that my husband was with someone else. I wasn't mad that he was, but I was angry that I wasn't mad.

That weekend with the girls was one of the best vacations of my life, and I needed it more than I really let on. Teresa had commented on our ride back into the city that she'd noticed my phone hardly rang. She said, "Gregory hasn't called much. He must know you're in good hands with me." He'd been busy in good hands, I'm sure.

And there was Miesha, a very young and beautiful Jamaican woman. We'd met at work, and I assumed I was at least 15 years older than her. The very first time I met her, I thought to myself, *This girl is rude!* I'd gone down to her department to check on a patient's insurance.

She never once looked up to acknowledge that I was there, and her tone was firm. But I saw something else in her that day: her heart, and she reminded me of myself. Not in physical appearance, but in spirit. I gazed at her face on that day, and I wondered if she knew how beautiful she was. I didn't think she did because of the way she avoided eye contact. I didn't see the confidence that I'd displayed in life, but I knew that she would be my sister. It took a few weeks to break the ice, but once we started to talk, I could see myself in Miesha. I wanted to save her from herself. I wanted to heal every wound that she'd ever had. I love her to this day, just as much as I love my sister in whom I shared a bed with for over 15 years. With her there were no secrets. Like Grisel, I was able to be honest with her without judgement. As the years passed, our friendship grew and blossomed into something so magical that I can't find any words to truly describe it. When she was angry, her Jamaican accent would overwhelm me as I tried patiently to follow along. I tried to deposit as many valuable things into her because she had so much more time if she started now. She was only 22 years old. I didn't want her to become me and pretend to have a perfect life. I wanted her to create her very own perfect life—one just like my parents.

I didn't want to leave Boston but needed to go. My ex-husband denied that the baby was his up until the divorce. When I look back, it all makes sense. I would have received alimony for his child out of wedlock. He was now parading around town with his new family, and even though our divorce was final, I still hadn't told my parents or associates. Soon teachers and friends saw him with his new family. Many thought that the young girl was a family member or one of my daughter's friends because she looked that young. I was ashamed and disappointed. I was ashamed to tell my parents because they had wanted me to have a happy family. They had known way before I did that my ex-husband was having many affairs with local women. But they loved me too much to hurt me, and my mom still lived by her saying that a mother must do what she must do to keep her family, which included ignoring little things. I needed to find someone else to keep my mind off the demise of my family.

I decided to go online and search for a new lover. One thing that I'll never do again is look for someone else before being done with the previous relationship. I was divorced, but I was not done with my ex-husband. I had not forgiven him or myself, so I was living as a slave in my own mind. I was a captive of unforgiveness, and I continued to seek help from God and professionals. I visited the library almost every day, reading every self-help book that I could find. I began to apply them in my life and, over time, I started to feel better, not totally, but better.

Adjusting to life in Boston without James was difficult. We talked almost every day, and my parents loved having him in the house. My mom and James were exceptionally close. She said that he'd told her secrets that he'd harbored in his heart concerning his dad and me, but out of love and respect she could not talk about them with me. School had started already in South Carolina, so he complained that he didn't get a real break. He tried out for the basketball team, and when he made varsity during his freshman year, I was elated. I continued to study and seek God. I also began to prosper in areas of my life that I had spoken of as being good fortune. I was in the top of my class and would be graduating the following year. I began to talk to my parents about the truth of my life. I was honest with them about my involvements, too. They didn't judge me at all; instead, they encouraged me to repent, ask for forgiveness, and move on. It was easy to say, but so very hard to do. I tried my best to forgive my ex-husband and myself. All my married life, I made the excuse that I would take on other lovers because he had done so. But the more I rationalized the idea, it was me, and me alone, who decided to do the things that I did, and so I would have to forgive myself first.

I decided to date online because I wanted to be able to choose up front the type of man that I wanted. I'd never done it before, but my friend Teresa told me about so many success stories that friends of hers had online. There were physical attributes that I thought I needed back then: he needed to be tall, very tall, and athletic. He'd be the total opposite of my ex-husband physically, but also mentally and spiritually. I needed a man who adored his mother, one who would pray with me a few times a day, and was educated. I read a lot, so I needed someone who I could talk to about world events, politics, and even religion. These were the things that I thought I needed back then. What I really needed was the word of God. I needed to seek

God during those times, yet I stayed on familiar ground. I did what I had always done: look for a man to help ease the pain of loneliness.

If I could do it all over again, I'd shut down to the world and just open myself up to God. I'd get to know him so personally that I could see his face and hear his voice with clarity. I'd listen for his perfect will over my life so that I could walk in complete peace and love.

Hindsight is always so clear, and I converted to what had worked for me in the past. Just a short time after my divorce, I met a young African. His profile listed all the initial requirements that I had created. He was six foot seven inches tall, dark, and athletic. His profile stated that he loved his mom more than anything. I sent him a message, and he responded within minutes. Then we exchanged numbers.

Madou and I arranged our first date after talking for only a few weeks. We met at a small coffee shop in Harvard Square. We talked for hours. He'd been an immigrant from a small country in West Africa. He grew up very poor, which fueled his ambition to come to the U.S. and live the American dream. We had so much in common it was strange. You never think that your life mirrors that of someone from another country with different cultures. One thing that I learned during my years in Boston was that we are all way more alike than we are different. There are only a few superficial things that make us different, but most of us share that commonality of wanting to be loved. We're spiritual beings created in love, so it's our spiritual nature to seek it. But we must know that God will provide the love that will complete us. For me on that night, Madou would suffice.

We talked for hours until the staff of the small coffee shop started cleaning the tables and floors around us. They did not disturb our intense conversation. We talked about religion, and neither he nor I was excited about man-made religions, preferring a personal relationship with God. He was a Muslim by birth, and I had been a Christian. But neither of us were moved by the only difference that we discovered on that night. Instead, we both concluded that there is but one God. He'd call him Allah and I'd call him God, which all in all meant the same thing. Because I've always been so confident in myself, I've never been the one to put another person down if their beliefs did not coincide with mine. I didn't judge others for their sins because I didn't know the sins of others. I only knew my own, and that's all I needed to know. I could only ask God to forgive my sins, not another's. There was no need for me to judge or dwell on others. I didn't want to leave Madou on that night, all the while knowing that I had to go back home to face my own issues.

For the next few months, I worked, studied, spent time with my daughters, visited my son in South Carolina as often as I could, and I got to know Madou. The more that I got to know about him, the more I liked about him. I didn't want to get into a sexual relationship with another man right away. I'd played too many of those games in the past. I told him that I'd taken a vow of celibacy for a year. He said that it was not a problem for him. I hadn't taken any vow. My purpose was to see if he was just looking for sex or for a solid relationship as his online profile stated. It seemed to me as though he was truly seeking a relationship. We dated for a few months, enjoying dinner and movies often. He enjoyed cooking, so most evenings he'd cook dinner at his place. I spent lots of time there.

The winter of 2011 was the perfect time to spend cuddled with a new lover. It was our first weekend that we'd planned to spend together because my daughters were going away with their grandparents. Then came a bad snowstorm. The roads to Lynn where Madou lived were closed. I didn't know what to do. I did know that I didn't want to be alone with the kids gone. I had to get there. I called Madou to see if he knew any shortcuts, but he didn't. He suggested that I ride the train and walk the three miles to his house. He would walk there and meet me because his car was snowed in. He and I were both in really good shape physically, so the distance wasn't a problem at all. I hopped on the red line train station at Central Square and headed to Lynn.

Madou was waiting at the station, with his tall frame hovering over the others walking about the station. It was brutally cold, and the snow was piling up quick. The walk seemed to take forever, and it felt like my nose was going to freeze off. My legs weren't tired because they were so strong from all of my running and weight training. When Madou picked me up and carried me for a few blocks, I thought I'd pass out from shock. For one, I was fit but I wasn't small—a solid 160 pounds. I'd never had anyone carry me before. In his beautiful thick African accent, he whispered, "You're not too heavy but your burdens are. Don't bring them this weekend, and let's just enjoy each other." I had thought that I'd done a good job not showing him how broken I was. I thought that I'd done a good job pretending that life was perfect. I think I fell in love with Madou on that night or had the thought of falling in love with him.

Our relationship changed on that weekend. He became my lover, but unlike any other lover that I'd had in my past, he was the first lover that I'd taken as a single woman. With him I wasn't revenge cheating on my husband. I wasn't trying to fill a void that the man I was married to had created. I felt free for the first time in a very long time. I was free from infidelity, dishonesty, and loneliness with unforgiveness pending. Madou was six years younger than me and he'd never been in a long relationship, so he harbored an innocence that was so beautiful like breathing fresh beach air.

During the following spring, we talked about marriage and children. Not marriage between the two of us, as we hadn't quite gotten there yet, but these things in general. He told me that in his family the marriages were usually arranged, and he would have to marry a Muslim woman. He asked me would I ever consider converting. I didn't realize that he followed his family traditions. He had been away from his family for more than a decade and seemed just as American as me. He also talked about the men having more than one wife back home in his country.

I wasn't totally against his traditions, and I truly meant it when I said that I don't judge others when it comes to their way of life. I started to feel that Madou wouldn't be my husband because of those simple things that made us so different, but he said that he didn't have to follow the African traditions because he was not there. I saw the conviction in his eyes when talking about the importance of pleasing his parents. I knew first-hand how important that was because I'd spent my entire life trying to please my parents.

My mom had casually taken my place in my son's life. He loved her so much, and she adored him. I remember when he and I had shared that same relationship. I still adored him more than anything in this world, but he hadn't totally forgiven me for not staying with his father. He was too young to truly understand the perfect life that I'd tried to create for him. He'd been too young for me to even share those types of secrets so I suffered through the feeling of not being adequate.

On the day before I was scheduled to leave for South Carolina, I called him to confirm the place of the basketball game. I was going to get to Florence at six o'clock and rent a car at the airport and drive to Hartsville by seven o'clock. My dad said that he planned on going to the game. My dad would never miss a game. From middle school, all the way through high school, I cannot remember him not being there for any of my games. I thought about how proud my son must feel to have my dad in his life. My dad made you feel proud. I've learned through the years that we shouldn't talk so much about it; we should just be about it. That's how my dad was. You'd never heard him use any adjectives to describe himself, but he was honest, supportive, loving, kind, God-fearing, genuine, faithful, and trustworthy.

When I arrived at the gymnasium that evening, I saw the green and gold uniforms huddled to the side of the court. I got there just in time for tipoff. James looked so big and strong. He'd grown a few inches since I last saw him. I couldn't believe that my baby was playing varsity basketball in only the ninth grade. I had talked to his coach on the telephone and when I saw him, his voice matched his firm build. I looked around for my dad and found him anxiously waiting for the game to begin. He was wearing a team jersey, and when he saw me, I saw that gleam of joy in his eyes. The way this man loved me was almost surreal. I hugged my dad and shouted for my son's team. He looked up, and our eyes met, and it was in that moment that I found magic. It was in that moment that I thanked God for the opportunity. Some things that we take for granted when we have everything become small miracles when we have nothing.

I enjoyed that weekend so much. I slept in my old room with my son. It was only a twin bed in there, the same bed that I'd slept on more than a decade ago. I remember cuddling so tightly with him. I remember praying with him, and I didn't want to leave him.

On the Sunday that I was supposed to leave, I watched him cry for me. I hadn't seen him cry in such a very long time that I didn't want to leave him there. I knew that he was in a good place, but when a parent is without their child, it's hard to see the good. That flight back to Boston was the longest ever. I decided on the ride back that I'd have to get back to South Carolina. I needed to be there with my son. I couldn't see my future in Boston without him, and I wanted to be near my parents.

For the first time in a long time, other than missing my perfect life, I was happy. And it wasn't about meeting a man. I was happy that I was finally making decisions that weren't based on revenge or perception. I began to desire a pure life rather than a perfect one. I wanted a pure life with God. I went about my quest in the months that followed my return from South Carolina. I began working first on the image that I saw in the mirror. Truth be told there were things about myself that I really didn't like. Some of them had been planted in my head by my ex-husband. To men, my physical appearance was appealing, but I noticed that my husband never took a lover with similar physical attributes as me. He'd always take to women with light skin, women without curves, or women with small features. It caused me to second guess the beauty that my mother had spent years assuring me was without a doubt flawless. I began to work out every day, sometimes twice a day. I started my first wellness program. I wanted to feel my best, and I wanted to help others along the way.

I am thankful that in all my pain and hurt I've been blessed with a helping spirit. It's one of the reasons Mother Teresa has always been one of my role models. I admire the way she gave without expectation. I love the way she met the lost and broken right where they were. She found no need for lavish things for herself as she journeyed out into some of the harshest parts of the world, and she took nothing with her but love. She didn't stay in any of the hotels and slept in the villages of those she was trying to save. And I'm not talking about beautiful huts and tropical islands, I'm talking about some of the poorest parts of the world, where there was no clean drinking water, no electricity, and no beds. I'd often wonder where does a person gets such drive to help others without expectation? I would later learn from God alone.

My wellness program was a huge success among my close friends. I had transformed my great body into a masterpiece, and others wanted to join in. We met three days a week and we followed an eating plan that cut out carbohydrates while increasing our fruits and vegetables. Within six months, my team had lost a whopping 280 pounds of fat. I also had a new man in my life who seemed to adore my success and encouraged me to do more. I began to pray and fast more. I prayed like the Muslims, five times a day. I read the Bible at night, and I fasted for a week at a time when the pressures of life or the embarrassment of my past resurfaced. My fasting was pure: I did not eat or drink for seven days. I didn't tell others when I was fasting; I just pretended that I'd already eaten.

My daughters were both playing basketball. Coaching girls' basketball in Cambridge fitted perfectly into my perfect life back then. I started out by helping the head coach the first year that we'd moved to Cambridge. He was a good coach, but provided only skills and missed when it came to self-esteem building and improving social skills. I think that during my first year helping with the team he was going through a divorce. He announced that he wouldn't be coming back to the team the following year, and something inside of me said that this was my opportunity. I worked full-time, but I knew that I could fit the time in during the season. I approached the principal and she stated that I had already been recommended. I went into work and explained to my director that I loved my job, but this coaching job would complete me. I negotiated a schedule that allowed me to work early on Tuesdays and Thursdays so that I could make practices. I also took Friday afternoons off during the season for games.

I loved being with the girls. They were just as diverse as the community that we lived in. My point guard Sam was a petite Asian who had some of the most developed ball-handling skills I'd ever seen for a middle-schooler. My starting guard Claudia was a quick Cape Verdean who had an amazing jump shot, and my center was a tall and strong Haitian named Clara who I loved like my own daughter. My power forward Rose was a lean African, and my second forward Tiffany was an Irish beauty who transformed into a beast on the court.

My oldest daughter played forward, while my youngest prepared to join the team the following year. These young ladies became my second group of daughters, and they each looked up to the woman that I displayed to them. I taught them to not only be strong athletes but to be strong young women. I know some of them got these teachings at home, but I enforced them outside of the home. I became an auntie to most of the girls, not really a mom, but a young auntie, and they could come to me with anything. I did not judge or scorn them, and planted seeds of honesty. I promised them that anything they told me stayed between only us, and I'm proud that I kept my word. There was only one time that I had to go against my word, and I don't regret it, because I know that it was totally necessary.

Jessica had not been the most skilled player on the team, but she hustled like you wouldn't believe. I mean she was always running. She ran to the locker room, to get water, to get anywhere. When she was on the court, you'd never see her just standing still. She was always moving, even if she was just jumping in place.

I used Jessica as an example for the team when it came to hustle. I'd lived my entire life on the pretense of perception, so I taught my team some of these things:

- ✓ No matter how weak we are, we must always appear strong.
- ✓ When we walk into the gym, we will walk like stallions.
- ✓ When we're on the court, we're always to look hungry— hungry for the ball, hungry for the next basket, and hungry for the win.
- ✓ When there was a timeout, I wanted all of them to run to the huddle and make some noise on the way.

Jessica had these things down pat. Her mom Mary was always at the games. Mary was a tall, beautiful woman who looked to be about my age, which meant that she, too, had been a teen mom. We talked often and she mentioned that she noticed some changes at home with Jessica and asked if I'd noticed any. I hadn't. Jessica continued to be her energetic self, leading the team in steals even though she hardly took a shot.

But on the night of our first playoff game, I noticed right away that Jessica was different. She didn't run in, just slowly walked in. I immediately asked if she was okay, and she said that she dreaded the end of the season because she would have to start going back over to her grandparents' house after school. She said that, during the season, she stayed late at school and rode home with one of the other girls and stayed at her house for an hour until her mom got home. I knew about this arrangement because her mom requested in writing that she was to leave practices with the other young girl's mom.

The girls always kept me busy during the season, and I didn't have time to worry about what young woman my husband was having an affair with, and I didn't have time to pick up another affair of my own.

During the basketball season, I was happy. It hadn't dawned on me that my husband had never come to a game. The rival girls' coach walked in with her husband and two young kids. They sat directly behind her as she coached the girls on to the city championships, leaving us as the runners-up. I noticed that my husband never saw me in this beautiful place, and it hurt.

But my hurt was overshadowed when Jessica began to tell me why she didn't want to go to her grandparents' house. Before she began to talk, she asked "Coach, will you promise not to tell anyone what we talk about?" I reassured her that I'd never violate her trust, and I loved her like my own child. She continued with the fact that her grandparents were two of the most beautiful people she knew. They had helped raise her when her parents divorced.

About two years ago their son, her Uncle Mike, moved back from Georgia to live with them. Mike was smart and funny and worked as an IT specialist and knew everything about computers. But Jessica noticed early on that he was very touchy. He always found a way to touch her. She hadn't thought much of it because she noticed that he did the same thing with others, even her mom. She figured her Uncle Mike was just one of those people who talked with their hands.

Last spring, Jessica said that her grandmother became ill and was admitted into a hospital. Her grandfather stayed at the hospital with her grandmother, and she went over there with her Uncle Mike after school until her mom got off from work. She had asked her mom if she could just stay home alone, but her mom didn't trust the neighborhood or the people and needed to know that she was safe.

"But Coach, I'm not safe there." We both began to cry. I knew that I couldn't keep the secret that she was about to share with me. I also knew that this was going to be that exception.

Jessica said that on the third day of her grandmother's hospital stay, her uncle came upstairs to the room that was hers as a little girl. She was studying for a test. She noticed right away that he locked the door behind him. "Uncle Mike, why did you lock the door?" She then said that she saw something different in his eyes, something sick and perverted, and she knew that he was going to rape her. She said that she knew it before he even touched her. As he walked to the end of the bed, she said that she sat up quickly and begged him to leave. He said, "I promise you that I won't hurt you. It's time for you to feel a man, and I want to be the one to show you how a man feels. I'm your uncle and I love you."

Jessica said that he caused her so much pain during the first rape that she passed out. He bit her so hard on her back that she could hardly touch the bruise. He continued to rape her for the next year every chance he got. She became a pretender, acting like it never happened. She ran everywhere with a smile on her face so that no one would uncover her disguise.

I'd done the same thing for many years, so I understood her plight. I held her in my arms on that day and we cried together. She asked if she could come over to my house after school with my daughter who was also her friend. I told her she could but that wouldn't stop her uncle from finding the opportunity to hurt her again. People are that way. They will find an opportunity to do whatever it is that they want to do, including hurting others. I prayed for her on that night, but I also asked for guidance for myself. I could never live with such a secret. I would have to find a way to tell her mother.

I called her mother Mary the very next day and asked if we could meet for dinner and drinks. I told her that I wanted to talk with her, but she could not tell her Jessica that we were meeting. We met at the Hong Kong restaurant in Harvard Square. It was early and hadn't gotten packed yet. We ordered drinks and dinner. I didn't have an appetite, just needed a drink to give me the courage to say to her what was happening to her daughter.

She began to cry as soon as I started to ask, "How well do you know your younger brother Mike?" She pleaded with me, "Please tell me he hasn't touched Jessica. I've asked her repeatedly, and she says no." I told her that Jessica had confided in me about her secret, but it was her job now to protect her daughter. She confessed that her brother had been accused of molesting his ex-girlfriend's daughter in 1998, but the woman dropped the charges.

I cried with her, and I learned a valuable lesson about not trusting anyone. I made a promise that I would never bring a man around my daughters. I would not date inside my home. I would keep them safe.

The next year, Jessica returned to the team, and one afternoon after practice, she asked if she could talk to me. We hadn't spoken about it since that first day she told me. I had followed up with her mom who assured me that she was taking care of everything and that her brother would never again hurt her daughter. On that afternoon after practice, she said only five words, "Thank you for saving me." I started to believe that she told me because she knew that I would help her. She asked for secrecy because she didn't want me to discuss it prematurely, but she wanted me to help her.

4

The Shift

I'm now in this place and life feels good. My daughters are beautiful smart and healthy, and my only son is thriving and growing into the young man that I wanted him to become. And Madou still adores me. We've grown together in the past year. We don't talk religion because it's the only thing that divides us. We do pray together, but he ends his prayer with "Allahu Akbar," which means "God is the greatest." I'm totally okay with that because I agree wholeheartedly that God is the greatest.

We're spending so much time together, and I'm falling for him so hard, that I've almost forgot that, on the other side of town, the man to whom I had given my entire life to was living with a 21-year-old kid and her mother and his child out of wedlock. I had almost forgotten that he turned me into an adulterous woman who lived to avenge his wrongdoings.

Madou brought me joy. He made me smile, and I was excited about showing him to the world. Yes, many people didn't know that I was divorced already, but they'd find out soon enough because we were getting ready for the wedding of one of my colleagues. It was going to be a very extravagant wedding, and every one of my friends from work would be there. I called one of my dearest friends who is also a fashionista to help me pick out an outfit for the occasion. Elizabeth was one of the most fashionable people that I'd ever met. I presumed that she looked elegant even in her sleep. I've never seen her looking less than fabulous. She grew up in Paris, and her father, a Haitian diplomat, taught her that she was to always look distinguished—and this she did.

We went to the mall on the Saturday before the wedding and Elizabeth helped me pick out the most beautiful dress. She said that I should go with a streamlined dress to accent my hips. I said, "Okay."

Later, I showed Madou the dress, and he was impressed. Ever so more impressed when I arrived at his place the next Saturday wearing this beautiful dress with hints of gold lining my eyes and lips. He said that I looked perfect. And he was perfect for me at that time. Although I wore six-inch heels, he still hovered over me. His beautiful black skin was radiant under the shea butter that he applied to his body. He was my African prince for the night.

On the ride to the wedding, I felt nervous. This was the first time in my life that I'd been out at an event with anyone other than my ex-husband. I hoped that people who didn't know wouldn't ask too many questions. We entered the reception looking like a couple that belonged in *Ebony* or *Jet*. My co-workers didn't ask any questions, and I guess they all had already discussed the demise of my perfect life.

I learned later that my manager had a half-cousin who while dating had a baby with an older married man. To his surprise when he went to the child's first birthday party, he learned that the man was my ex-husband. He was hurt and disgusted, but he and the rest of my team felt sorry for me. They didn't know that I had condoned such behavior leading up to this situation, and that I, too, had taken other lovers without remorse.

Even big cities are like small towns, as things get out because we're more connected to others in this world than we think. Most of my colleagues were happy to see me looking so happy with such a tall, handsome, intelligent man on my arm.

The bride came over and gave me a hug and said that she had been praying for me and she was happy that I'd met someone—all of this after calling my ex-husband a "scum-bag" for leaving me. What many people didn't know is he didn't just leave me, he never really committed to me at all; it was just an illusion that I had created.

We danced late into the night. I drank wine and enjoyed the joyous occasion for my coworker. Madou didn't drink and didn't mind that I enjoyed mixed drinks. For me, he bought wine and kept it at his place for my stressful evenings. It was on this night that he told me for the first time that he loved me, and I believed him because I loved him, too. I wished that this was the end to a perfect love story. I wished that he would be the man who I loved. I wished that he desired only me…not to be. I love Madou to this day, but it was not in God's will that he be that man for me.

Our love affair world-winded. We were together almost every day. He had a very busy work schedule, but he fit me in nicely. I noticed that I was spending a lot of time away from my daughters. My oldest was 15, and she could stay at home alone with her younger sister. I decided that it was time that the kids met Madou. I planned for it to happen at dinner the next Thursday. I explained to the girls that I cared about him and he was good to me. Surprisingly, they were both thrilled. He was a little hesitant about meeting them, and I understood because he was such a young man that it might be overwhelming to think about being a stepfather to teenage girls.

When he arrived for dinner, he was dressed in one of his black suits and a beautiful blue silk shirt. He took his shoes off at the door, which hadn't been a requirement for us, but it had become a way of life for him. I tried to break the ice over dinner, but neither he nor the girls talked much. They kept answering me with yes or no. I guess I didn't ask enough open-ended questions.

My oldest daughter asked him a few questions about his culture. He went on to talk about his childhood. He spoke about his mother and father's arranged marriage and the "bride price." This was the first time that I'd heard him talk about a "bride price." I was just as interested as my daughter. After dinner, I walked him to the car, and asked him what did he think? He said that he thought I was an amazing mom and that my daughters would grow up to be just as amazing as I was. I prayed that night that they wouldn't grow up and become me. For them, I prayed for pure happiness and love. I prayed that they would never have to pretend for a society of people that really didn't need their lies or cared if they were perfect or not.

Things changed a little between Madou and me, but not enough to cause alarm. He was planning a trip back to his country, and I was excited for him. I wished that he'd asked me to come along, as I would have jumped at the opportunity to visit West Africa. On the week that he was planning on traveling back home, I planned another trip to South Carolina to visit my son. I didn't feel comfortable enough yet to tell him about the new man in my life. I'm sure his sisters had told him that they'd met him. He and his sisters were close, as I'd raised them that way. Yes, they had the sibling quarrels, but when push came to shove, they took care of each other.

My visit to South Carolina was a good one. I didn't take the girls and instead dropped them off with their grandparents. I told them that soon we would all go back to South Carolina and they were excited. I spent the entire trip with my son. We went to the movies and dinner. We went to a baseball game with my dad, and we went shopping. I was beginning to fall in love with the south again. Each visit made me think about being near the beach, walking barefooted on the dirt roads. I have so many sweet memories on a dirt road. Sometimes, it's in the simplest of things that you find the most joy.

On my last day there, I took off my shoes and headed toward the road. My son followed, and I remember the smell of the earth and playing hide and seek in the cornfields to the left. For that moment, I was back in time, just 10 years old, and I didn't have to pretend that my life was perfect. It was perfect.

I returned to Boston on the same day I returned to work. I always wanted to get as much time with my son as possible, so my flight arrived at Logan Airport at seven in the morning, and I hopped on the bus and then the red line train that took me straight into Harvard Square. Carrying my small luggage, I walked the half a mile to work. I was out of vacation time, so I needed to get back to work. I'd taken a lot of time off from work during my divorce. It was hard to think clearly during that time. The depression came in bouts, and it was vigorous. I'd have to take a few days off here and there, which was not a problem because during the days of my perfect life, I was never out of work. I accumulated so many sick days and vacations days that I thought to cash them out all at once. I'm glad I didn't because I needed them during those dark days.

When I walked into the office, it was already busy, and I went straight to work. I was there working, but my mind was all over the place. I was back in South Carolina with my son. I was in West Africa with Madou. I was sitting on the end of my bed looking through old family pictures. My mind was everywhere on that day, but my body was sitting there in my office going over admissions paperwork. I said a quick prayer for God to help ease my mind so that I could focus on the workday.

I was interrupted in thought by my close friend Teresa. She tapped on the door and came right in. She wanted to know the details of my trip, and she also wanted to know about my new man after seeing him at the wedding. The entire office wanted details, but she was the only one who could come to me for them. I loved her like a sister, but I didn't want to talk about it too much in case it didn't work out. I told her that Madou was an amazing man and we'd already shared "I love you," but I wasn't sure where we were headed, as he was much younger. Teresa giggled, "Age ain't nothing but a number."

A few minutes later, our director stepped in, "You guys can catch up later. There are patients waiting." I continued to work with my mind all over the place, and yet no one knew that but me. I'd become a pro at making things look the way I wanted them to appear. I walked home that afternoon in tears. I cried because I missed my perfect life, and I cried because there was something inside telling me that something bad was coming. I didn't know what, but it made me sad.

Madou returned the following week, and he looked rejuvenated. He was so happy to see his family after so many years. He talked vividly about his country and the beauty of West Africa. He said that he wasn't totally in agreement anymore with a lot of the old traditions. He talked about being bathed by the elders with some homemade herbs that would make him fertile. The elders were concerned because he was 28 years old and had not wed yet. They believed that the ceremony would bring him a wife and many children.

It was so beautiful to hear about his country and what was more enticing was the way he looked when he recalled his time there. I saw a spark in his eyes that I'd never seen before. I wanted to be there with him. How wonderful it would be to live in Africa with the beauty of nature, with modest things, and just live a perfect life. Then reality hit me: I couldn't move my kids across the world, and they wouldn't even want to go.

Madou and I spent the weekend together just talking. We cooked traditional West African dishes for dinner. He brought me a few things, one of which was bark from a tree that is used to clean teeth. He said that it's much better than a toothbrush. He said it was the reason why he and his people had the whitest teeth. I had to agree, and I used it for a few weeks. I didn't notice much difference in my own teeth, so I just put it aside. On the Sunday of his return, we started to talk again about religion. I stayed away from these kinds of conversations with him because it was one of the things that we didn't agree upon. Why waste time on our differences when we had so much in common?

He said that it is very important to his family that he marry a Muslim woman, but for him it was not that important. He said that if I wasn't Muslim that I would have to convert on the day of the wedding. Is he talking marriage? Was I in love with this beautiful Muslim man? He'd shown me nothing but love for the past year. Not once did he make me feel inadequate, and not once had I cheated on him. He made me faithful. When we were together at his place, he always kept his cellphone visible. If it rang, he'd casually ask me to hand it to him if it was near me. I always felt secure with him, especially when we were cuddled on the living room couch watching the Boston Celtics play. I told him I needed to think about it, but I could never renounce my God, and I knew that in his heart he knew that.

We didn't bring up the conversation about marriage again after that day. I wanted to, but I thought the ball was in his corner. He had to have known how much I loved him. I continued to plan my move back to South Carolina without often considering our relationship for some reason. I often thought that if he loved me enough, he'd come with me. I heard him complain too much about the winters in Boston and how beautiful he thought the south was after I returned and talked about my recent visits with my son and parents.

I was now preparing for my final year in school, and I was looking forward to having my parents see me walk across the stage and get my second college degree. It had been their hearts' desire since the day that I was born. I had lived my life trying to show my parents that I had a good life. I wanted them to know that the decisions that I made early on to become a teenage mom and get married had not been in vain. But now as the time was approaching, I was beginning to feel as though I had disappointed them. They wanted only the best for me, and here I was divorced with three kids, a Muslim boyfriend, and an ex-husband who'd gone out and gotten a girl pregnant who was just a few years older than our oldest daughter.

When I look back now, it was pure shame. But I was still excited at least I could bring them some joy. I booked their flights the week before my final exams. My parents and my son would be here the day after Memorial Day. I called my mom after I booked the flight and gave her the itinerary. They'd be flying out of Myrtle Beach and directly into Boston. My girlfriend agreed to meet them at the airport because I was working. I also told my mom about Madou. I told her that I'd met him shortly after my divorce. I told her that he cared for me, and he made my life easier. She was quiet for a while then she began, "It's too soon for you to be in another relationship. You were married all of those years to one man, and you just don't move on from that so soon."

Time was really moving fast. I finally got a chance to talk to Madou about my plans. He asked me if I was serious about moving back home. I told him that I was, but I didn't tell him my total reasons for leaving. Though I was finally in a healthy relationship with a man who seemed to adore me and believed in fidelity, I was still heartbroken. I could hardly stand risking the chance of running into my ex-husband and his child lover and their kid—and I ran into them often. We lived only 15 minutes apart, so I ran into them at the supermarket, the mall, and even the gym. It was always awful, and I turned around and ran out no matter where we were. I tried to stay on the Eastside of town because that's where I saw them the least. I remembered the last time that I saw them together. He was so smitten over the child that he didn't even look up. He was doting on her, and she was beautiful. I remembered the many times he denied that the child was even his but, on this day, there was no doubt that he was in love. I never remember him being so in love with any of my kids, not even our son. I didn't feel jealous, just pure anger. I wished again on that day that the child would just die, and I then could go and get my family back. If the child was gone, we could start all over again. I didn't mind if he took new lovers. I just needed him to be careful and not have any more children. I cried terribly that night. I cried myself to sleep as all kind of crazy thoughts swamped my mind. *How could I even think such thoughts?* I was going crazy perhaps. I reached out again for help as I didn't want to lose my mind.

Madou said that he would start looking for a job in the Columbia area. He asked me what the financial district looked like in the capital city of South Carolina. I told him that I had no idea and needed to do some research. He sounded like he wanted to move with me. One evening as I was on his computer, I went back to the recent pages, and there were pages on "financial jobs in South Carolina" and "houses for sale in South Carolina." I felt overwhelmed with love on that day. I believed that Madou really wanted to be with me and to love me, and I hadn't felt this way in a very long time, though my heart was all over the place.

I started to plan my return to the Carolinas. I also started to work on healing myself of old hurt and limitations. The first thing that I had to change was caring so much about perception. I had to learn that things are hardly ever the way that they appear. I needed help to get through because those feelings that would stir up when I saw my ex-husband could not be normal. I mean, I had already moved on, and Madou was a great man. I called my primary care doctor and told him that I needed to speak with someone about my feelings of periodic despair. He referred me to a new therapist. Her name was Rachel and her office was located just two blocks off Central Square. You see I was seeking all sorts of help, but I had refused to go to the source. I didn't want to go to God for healing because I was ashamed. Back then, I thought somehow that if I went to God with all my wicked thoughts and ways, he would be so disappointed that he wouldn't help me. Crazy thinking, as if God didn't see and hear my every thought and every deed whether good or bad. I had convinced myself of these things, so I was being held captive in my own mind. I was seeking a freedom that I didn't really want. I had gotten so used to being bound in perception. We hear people say all of the time, "I wish that I knew then what I know now." I stopped saying this when I realized that the truth is always available, and we just choose to delay our knowledge of it.

One week later, I met with Rachel. She was a pleasantly plump lady with a seventies look. As a matter of fact, she made me feel as though I'd stepped back in time. I wondered how much mousse she had used to get her hair to stand up that tall. She was a young woman, though, and I would guess that she was only a few years older than me. Her dress had a real throw-back look and so did her platform heels.

She started by asking me the question that all medical doctors ask their patients: "So what brings you here today?" I did not know how to answer that question, so I remained silent for a few minutes. Rachel didn't rush me for the answer; instead she got up and went over to the round table in the corner and refilled her coffee cup. She didn't ask if I wanted any because I had my Dunkin Donuts coffee nestled tightly between my legs.

She broke the silence after a few minutes, "Dr. Ortiz says that you're struggling after a divorce and are in need of some counseling through the difficulties." I began to cry. You see, every time I thought about my perfect life ending in divorce I cried. She said that it was normal to cry. I said that I didn't understand how my ex-husband could have done this to me. She said that divorce was a death, and that many people grieved for years. *Is this lady crazy? Does she think I'm going to grieve for much longer? I'm going to get over this quick and create a new perfect life.* She said that we had an hour together, and I could talk to her about anything, but she first wanted to go into my childhood. She wanted to know what life was like for me as a child. I began to tell her how much my dad loved my mom, and how perfect he was to her. I told her about our daily dinners and how active my parents were in my social life. I spoke about the support of my father and, how he never missed a game. I told her how my mother built our confidence.

Then she asked a question that no one had never asked me: "Why do you feel so worthless right now?" I'd never displayed any characteristics of a worthless person. I'd always displayed those things that my mom had given me. I walked tall and strong, and I never showed anyone anything that would make them think that I felt worthless. But I did, and I didn't know how Rachel knew this. I felt worthless because I'd spent my adult life with a man who never loved me. Despite knowing early on, I couldn't disappoint my children or my parents, so I stayed and created a perfect life. He loved the idea of me, and I felt worthless for even begging him to marry me. You see it was not his idea to get married. I became pregnant, and he said that he'd take care of me and my daughter. I was too young to understand much, but I knew that unless he was my husband he was bound to leave. I begged him to marry me, "Make me your wife and make us a family." He got us a small apartment together because my mother had already told me, "No babies are coming into this house unless they come out of my belly." In other words, if you had a baby, you would have to take care of it on your own.

As soon as I moved to this apartment right after the marriage, warning bells began to ring all over the place. He disappeared for days and left me and my week-old child alone without a telephone. He returned as if he'd never left. I never really question him, as I was so young and naive, and I couldn't become a statistic, so I needed to keep my daughter's father in her life. I did all the things I could think of to make him happy. I was faithful to him back then. As a matter of fact, I couldn't even think of being with another man. I tried to talk to my mom once about it, and she was clear about her position: "Geneva, you do not want to be a single mom, so stay with him and don't upset him with allegations as long as he is providing for you and you have place to stay and he doesn't put his hands on you."

This was engraved in my mind. I would stay, but I felt so worthless because I could not be loved by him.

I didn't tell Madou I was getting counseling again. We were spending lots of time together, and he was planning to attend my daughter's first high school basketball game. Since the divorce, I tried to get her father to come, but he always said he was too busy working. I can imagine that it was hard providing for two families because, throughout it all, he continued to provide for us financially in his absence. I didn't give him any props for doing so. I mean he was living in a house with his young girlfriend and her immigrant mother, so he didn't have any real bills over there. Besides that's what he's required to do.

On the way to the game, Madou seemed very distant. I asked him if anything was wrong. He said that he'd acquired some extra pressures at work. He didn't want to talk about it, except to say he had a new client overseas who was difficult. I'd never been seen at the school with anyone other than my ex-husband, but the entire school had already heard of our divorce and most had seen him with his new family, so I thought it was about time. I mean I was proud to be seen with Madou, so I walked into the gym without hesitation or reservation. My daughter felt nervous, though. Madou had played basketball in college and he was good.

She had lots of nervous turnovers that night, but it felt like the old family times. My son called my cell phone while we were at the game. "Ma, what's the score?" I told him that they were losing bad and that I'd call him when the game was over. Madou and I waited at the car for my daughter and her friends to come from the locker room. They packed the back seat. Madou said, "I don't think it's legal or safe for six of them to squeeze back there." I'd done it so many times that I said, "We'll be fine. The first two kids live less than five minutes away from the school."

We dropped them all off, and I wondered if Madou was down for all of this. I mean, I had an already made family and my kids were my priority. He didn't seem to mind, but I asked him anyway when we got back to my apartment. He said on that night that it really didn't matter to him. I was such a wonderful woman and he thought that it was beautiful the way I loved my kids. We ended the night on that note, kissed, and said our goodbyes.

I continued to meet with Rachel twice a week for the next two months. She said that I'd grown tremendously, and I should continue to write in my journal. She suggested that I keep a journal and always speak against all negative things before they took root in my life.

On our last visit, she asked if I had a personal relationship with God. I quickly answered, "Of course I do. My parents raised me in the church." I wanted to ask her why she asked me that question, but I now know that it was divine. For my entire life, I had known God. I had prayed to him and petitioned him for things that I needed. As I walked home that day from my meeting with Rachel, I thought of what a personal relationship looked like. I had a personal relationship with my parents, with my children, with my ex-husband, with my lovers, and with Madou. In those relationships, we did things together, we talked to each other, and we shared things. I had not spent any time alone with God. I didn't hear from him or her. I only went to him when I needed something. On that day, I opened my mind to God. I opened my heart to him because I needed him and not just when I needed him. I needed him to be an ever-present friend in my life. I needed a personal relationship. I longed for it, and I began to seek his face like I'd never done before.

The counseling and the personal time alone were helping me get over the demise of my marriage. Madou helped immensely by showing me that he cared for me and letting me be faithful. It was easy to be faithful to him because he provided me all that I needed. It was also easier because I wanted to please God and make my personal relationship stronger with him. Madou had begun to work more hours than before. He said that things were getting harder back in his native country, and he needed to send more money to his family. I didn't see him as much, but when we were together, things were good. I stopped seeing things as perfect. Trying to be perfect had almost ruined my life. One Saturday morning, I received a text message from Madou that he would be off from work by five and needed to talk to me about something urgent. I started to get nervous. I replied, "Let's talk now." I mean it was only 10 o'clock, and he wanted me to wait all day to talk about something urgent. Madou was stern, and I knew that he couldn't be persuaded, so I agreed to meet for dinner at one of our favorite Thai restaurants. To keep myself busy, I asked the girls if they wanted to go to the movies. I would also call my son and talk to him for as long as he'd give me.

James was so busy in South Carolina that our conversations were usually quick. "I'm good, Ma. Granddad takes me here and there. We're playing cards now."

On this Saturday morning, he was sleepy when I asked him to wake up and talk to me. I wanted to hear about last night's game, and I wanted details. I wanted to tell him about my new relationship with Madou and how I thought things were headed towards marriage. After he told me about the game, he told me about this very pretty eleventh grader that he wanted to ask out. I got distracted with that and didn't get around to my planned conversation. Before I knew it, my dad was calling out to him to get ready. I asked him where he was going. He said that my dad was taking him to the YMCA this morning to play some pickup ball with kids from the nearby city.

5

Agonizing Pain

W̶hen Madou picked me up for our dinner date that night, he had a very distant look in his eyes—one that I had never seen before. I asked him, "Is everything okay" Are you healthy? Are you sick? Why do you seem so far away?" He said that he was fine physically and so was everyone else. He said, "We'll talk when we get there."

For the next 20 minutes, Madou and I drove in complete silence to the restaurant. No music or radio just complete silence. I didn't pray like I'd usually did when I felt something was wrong. I kept my mind open, and I didn't think about anything. It sounds weird, but I rode to the restaurant with a blank mind. Before he picked me up, I thought that maybe tonight would be the night that he would propose to me.

But when he got there, I saw the distance in his eyes, and I knew that this was not the case. I didn't allow him to come around to open my door when we got there; instead I jumped out and headed toward the restaurant door. He ran quickly behind me to catch up and didn't complain.

We were seated, and by the time the waiter came to take our order, I had lost my appetite. I had that very nervous feeling in my stomach that wouldn't allow me to put anything in there. He ordered roasted duck and vegetables, and I ordered soup.

"Are you not hungry?" he asked.

"No, I'm not that hungry, I'm just so anxious to know what has you so tense."

I knew that it hadn't been anything that I'd done, as the past year and a half had been magical. I'd always been honest and faithful. Yes, there were times when I didn't talk about the toll of the divorce on my life and being with him had even made that easier in some ways.

When his food arrived, he pushed it to the side. Apparently, he had that same nervous stomach because he didn't touch his food. He grabbed my hands and looked me directly in the eyes and confessed, "Geneva, I am getting married next Saturday." *Oh, my God, this cannot be real. Please Geneva, wake up you are dreaming!* I started to cry. I had never suspected that Madou was seeing anyone else. I had a key to his apartment, and I came and went freely. He didn't have any passwords or locks on his cell phone, and I'd answer his phone if he was in the shower or anything. He often left his phone home when he went to the gym. I hated when I'd call him for something and hear the phone ringing on the nightstand. He said he used his iPod to work out so didn't need the phone to distract him. Up until this point, I would have never guessed that he was seeing anyone else other than me.

Something was wrong here. Was this some cruel joke? I checked his eyes for a sign, but they were clear and so what he said was the truth. I asked him, "Why? Do you not love me? Did you ever love me?" *Was this all just an illusion, perhaps another perception that I had created in my own mind?* After a few minutes he spoke, never letting go of my hands. I tried to draw back, as I didn't want to touch him ever again. I wanted to run for my life.

Madou explained to me that his bride had been chosen for some time now. It was a marriage arranged by his family. She was African and Muslim, two of the criteria for his family. He said that he didn't love her yet, but he would have to marry her because there was no other choice. "What do you mean yet?" I screamed. I was screaming so loudly that everyone in the restaurant turned their attention to us.

Madou was a huge man, and I'd never heard him scream in all the time that we were dating. We'd never had an argument.

Our waiter began to slowly approach our table with a look of concern on his face, and he asked if everything was okay. I screamed at him, "Hell no! It's not okay!" I looked at Madou and saw the tears in his eyes. I got up and walked out. I waited at the car because it was just too cold to walk home. He quickly followed. He reached over to open my door, and he grabbed my lower back like he'd done so many times before the sweetest kisses, but he didn't kiss me. He simply looked into my eyes and whispered, "I'm sorry, Geneva."

On the ride home, Madou drove slowly, as he rambled on about his culture and heritage and how he would be an outcast if he didn't go through with the marriage. I didn't really hear what he was saying because my mind was moving at a hundred miles per hour. I'd spent all this marvelous time with a man and now he tells me he's marrying someone else. We had just talked about moving together to South Carolina. I shouted at him, "Madou, please shut up and pull the car over. I need to throw up!" As he pulled over, I flung the door open just in time for everything that I'd eaten earlier that day to come up. I felt hot and dizzy, and I began to cry even more.

He jumped out of the car and came around to the passenger side. I was almost home, so I jumped out and began to walk. He started walking behind me, and I could hear his voice, but the only words that I could decipher were "I'm sorry."

Finally, I stopped and turned around to face him. He looked different now. My tall, handsome king now looked like a foreign dictator who was about to destroy my entire life by enforcing a law from his country. I yelled "Why?" I didn't wait for him to answer before injecting, "Why would you say that you love me? Why would you say that you wanted to move to South Carolina with me? Why did you get involved in my daughters' lives? Why, Madou?"

I started to beat on his chest in anger, not because I wanted to fight him, but I thought that if I beat on him the answers to my questions would flow out more easily. I didn't hit him hard enough to hurt him, and he knew that. He never grabbed my hands, he just stood there and let me pound on his chest until I was tired.

He spoke softly, "Geneva, I do love you, but in my culture, I have no choice but accept the bride of my family. My heart is with you, and I love your daughters, but I cannot go against my family or Allah." He said that he never cheated on me and that he has not even seen his new bride in person. She was still back in his country and would be arriving two days before the marriage ceremony. I didn't understand all of this, but I believed him.

When he grabbed me in his arms, I didn't resist or push him away. Instead I leaned into his strong muscular frame and I cried. As the snow began falling harder around us, we stood there for what seemed like an eternity and cried together.

When I reached home, Madou turned back to get his car. He asked if he could come upstairs for a little while to talk more. I told him that there was nothing left to talk about. I needed to start my life over again. I needed God and God alone.

On that night, I prayed for my ex-husband, and my ex-lover. I prayed that they would find peace in the choices that they'd both made, and I prayed that I would find peace in their choices. Madou didn't call for a few days and when he did, I answered quickly. *Had he come to his senses and called off this arranged marriage?* No... he said that he called to check on me and to tell me that he would always love me. I didn't say much and just wished him well and hung up. I told the girls the next morning that as soon as they finished school in June we were moving back to South Carolina.

There is no way that I could stay in this city knowing that the two men that I'd love were now with other women. It just wouldn't work. I began packing and getting ready for the move. I decided to have a yard sale to get rid of the things in my place. I would drive a small U-Haul attached to my car, and my daughters and I would hit the road on July 1. That left me less than two months in the city that had brought me so much joy for many years. I needed desperately to get my life in order and to repent for my wrong doings and move on.

You see every deed that we do in this life, I now believe we will pay for in this life. I had been an unfaithful wife, and I blamed it on my ex-husband's infidelity when, in fact, it was my choice and my choice alone. It was only right that I pay for it, despite my being faithful to Madou and expecting him to be the same with me, he took on another bride. Some call its karma; for me, it's simply reaping what you sow.

One afternoon as I was cleaning out the clutter in the basement so that I could get rid of the junk and decide what was good enough for my yard sale, I became so sick that I couldn't breathe. It was so cold and musty in that basement that I couldn't make it back up the stairs to the kitchen for some fresh air or a drink of water. I felt the room spinning, and I tried to scream for help, and then realized that I was home alone because the girls were with their grandmother.

Finally, after about 20 minutes, the episode subsided, and I slowly walked upstairs and sat at the kitchen table. As I sat there for a few minutes, I realized that my monthly cycle had not happened. I've been pregnant three times, and I knew all too well that I was pregnant again—this time by a married man. No, he wasn't married when we conceived the child; in fact, I had been under the assumption that I would be his wife. But here I was 34 years old, with three teenage children, divorced, and now pregnant with a child whose father was married to a woman whom he'd just met a few weeks ago.

Suddenly, my mind started to rationalize everything in some sort of distorted way. Maybe this would be the perfect way to get back at my ex-husband. He had a child out of wedlock, so this new child that I was carrying would be payback to him. I mean if Madou really loved me, he'd take care of this kid, and his new African wife would have to just understand.

For the next few weeks, I went about my life with a feeling of complete dread. My daughters noticed quickly that I was starting to sleep a lot again. They contributed it to depression because during my most depressed days, I slept endlessly. I continued to work out and eat healthy so I didn't gain any weight. And I didn't talk to Madou. I refused to speak to him, and I didn't know when I would tell him about the pregnancy.

One evening I was taking a stroll through Central Square. I stopped at the crosswalk and waited for the light to change. I happened to look up and to my right as the light turned from yellow to red, there he was at the red light, and the beautiful woman in the passenger side of the car was without a doubt his new wife. She was young and beautiful. I didn't despise her the way that I had my ex-husband's young lover. She was just so beautiful, that I stood there in awe for a few seconds. Madou saw me, though I refused to look at him. I felt his eyes upon me. My heart ached so badly, I cried all the way home, and I made an erratic decision to terminate the pregnancy on that evening. I called the nearest Planned Parenthood Center and scheduled the appointment.

When I got to the clinic, the place seemed so dark and dreadful. The staff all had a hopeless look in their eyes, even when they smiled. I began to wonder why my ex-husband hadn't taken his young lover to an abortion clinic. This day was one of the darkest days of my life. The nurse who administered the IV said that it would be painless and that I would soon drift off to sleep. When I awoke, it would all be over. *Was it too late to run? Could I just get up off this table and go home?*

I woke up feeling weird and thirsty. I asked for something to drink, but was told I couldn't have anything for the next few hours. I laid there and cried. Sharp pains pierced my lower abdomen, I felt empty inside. There are not many words to describe a woman whose womb has been emptied by force. That feeling of emptiness that seeps into the soul is the worst thing ever.

I began to think about the time that I thought about aborting my firstborn. I thought that if I aborted the pregnancy, I could go on to college as planned. If it hadn't been for the fact that I was deeply in love with her dad, I might have done it. You see when you're in love, nothing else matters. I believed that by having his child he'd put me first. Somehow, I believed that he'd stop all the affairs and step up and become the man that I had always wished that he would've been.

But if I had aborted my firstborn, then I'm not sure how my life would have been. It was my firstborn who gave me the will to live. I had promised that I would never let her see me struggle. I would provide a perfect life for her, the same life I had been given as a child.

Yet here I was at 34 years old, sitting in the cold exam room of a Planned Parenthood with no one. Yes, I had my children, but they could never see this side of me. At registration, they stated that someone would have to pick me up, but I didn't have anyone. I mean, I had lots of good friends, and a handful of them who I knew I could trust, but I was too ashamed to ask any of them to pick me up. So instead of leaving in two hours, I was told that I'd have to wait four hours before I could call a taxi.

For the next four hours, I saw my life through many different eyes. I saw myself through my mother's eyes, and I thought how proud she must be to see me behaving like the strong confident woman that she raised. I saw myself through my children's eyes, juggling school and work and still not missing a basketball or volleyball game. I saw myself through my friends' eyes, and I was the person that anyone of them called if they needed help or advice. And then I saw myself through my own eyes, and I was just an adulterous liar—a woman who had lied about her entire life and relied on other people's opinions of her and was too afraid to face reality.

I cried for the next four hours and made a vow that I had to free myself of these lies. As usual, I called on God only when I was in trouble, and today I was in trouble. I cried out to him for help and began to pray. My circumstances didn't matter as I believed that he was available to me whenever I was in need—today, I was in need.

The next few days back at home were horrible. I took a few days off work before I scheduled the procedure and asked my children's grandmother to watch them for a few days because I was not feeling well. I wished that I had enough courage to tell her the truth: pregnant by a man who had married another woman while dating me and, instead of embarrassing myself, I went to an abortion clinic and emptied my womb. Yes, just like that.

Sometimes, we have to say things just the way that they are without downplaying issues. I wished that I'd picked up the phone and called my mother or my sister or one of my closest friends, but, instead, I decided that I could not live this way any longer and had to end my life because I'd taken the life of my unborn child. I was tired of pretending and needed to be free.

I heard all the whispers: *You are not and never were enough. How could you possibly spend more than half of your life with a man who was never faithful to you? What kind of woman are you to get pregnant by an African man whose culture prohibits him from being with you? What kind of example are you to your daughters? Don't you think that they are secretly watching you and they know how worthless and dirty you are?*

The voices got louder and wouldn't stop yelling at me. I couldn't take it anymore and decided that I would end it all tomorrow. Time to stop all the lies and deceptions. Find a way, I thought, to put an end to this mess and silence the voices.

I remembered when I left my husband the first time, one of my closest friends suggested that I get a gun for personal protection. Call her tomorrow, I decided, to see if I could purchase a gun now. The voices said that it was a good idea and an easier way out. But then I started thinking about my children's grandmother bringing them back home and dropping them off downstairs as she often did. They always waved goodbye to her from the window when they got upstairs.

Not this time, after they saw me all black and bloody. I could not do that to them. I wanted them to see me like in a peaceful sleep, so I decided to take an overdose. The voices didn't want me to overdose because it took too long. Worse, if I didn't die right away, then I would suffer. Why were these voices in my head every second? I alone had to make this decision. My life was ending and not theirs. They were simply uninvited guests who were occupying space in my mind, and though they seemed so willing to help me get this done, it was my decision.

Blowing my brains out would end all this pain. I received pain pills after the procedure, but I need something else. I had 21 Percocet pills, so I got online and googled *How many and what kind of pills cause immediate death?* Read the information, and knew that I needed more pills. The next morning, I called the abortion clinic and told them that I'd lost my pills and needed another prescription. They quickly complied, and soon I picked up a new bottle of pills.

Time had come to put an end to all the heartache and shame by taking all the pills on Friday. *Why not?* After school, the kids were going over to their grandparent's house to stay for the weekend. On Friday morning, I would call my ex-mother-in law and ask her to please bring the kids upstairs rather than letting them come up by themselves. I was worried about leaving my children without a mother, but the voices had already convinced me that the kids would be fine. In fact, my parents would take better care of them than I ever did. They reminded me of my seemingly perfect childhood and how my parents ensured that I was given all that they could give me. My mother had succeeded where I'd failed and that was in creating a perfect life without boundaries.

I called Shirley, my ex-mother in-law, as soon as I woke up the next morning. She sounded tired, as if she'd been up all night. I asked her if she was sure that it was okay for the kids to come over this weekend. Shirley was aging, but she was still a vibrant and very active 60-year-old. She said that she was looking forward to the weekend with the kids.

I remained upbeat and told her that I was going to my friend's house for the weekend and asked her if she could bring the kids upstairs instead of dropping them off. I think my request sounded weird because she didn't reply. I continued, "I may not be back until late, and I want them to bath and be ready for school on Monday morning. So, if you could please come up and get them started with all of that, I'd be very grateful."

She was an amazing grandmother, and she'd come over and make sure that the kids were doing everything that they needed to do, including chores. In a weak moment, I thought ex-husband's lover had made a good decision in having a child with him because his parents would be more than just grandparents; they would help her and her child in any way possible.

6

The Little Girl Within

As soon as the kids walked out of the door for school, I called my office and told the secretary that I was sick and would not be in today and possibly tomorrow. She sounded concerned as I put on my sick voice, the one that everyone uses when calling out sick because of other plans like a long weekend on the beach, or a steamy evening out with a new lover, or too much partying too hard the night before and now the hangover was riding their back. I told her that I had some weird virus and was going to see my doctor tomorrow if the nausea and dizziness didn't subside.

I hung up and took the first bottle of pills very quickly. The voices kept taunting me to get it over with quickly because the longer I waited, the harder it would get. I waited only a few minutes before opening the second bottle of pills. I was beginning to feel dizzy and the furniture in the living room was moving around all over the place.

I got up to go into the bathroom. The voices said that I should lay in the tub, maybe even fill it with water just in case the pills took too long. I didn't fill the tub with water because I was too weak to turn the faucet knobs. Still, I laid down in the cold and wet bathtub. The bathroom felt like a freezer, and I wanted to get up and turn the heat on. Maybe I should die more comfortably. The voices commanded me to relax. I struggled to open the other bottle. My hands felt wet, and I was so cold.

As soon as I got the bottle opened, I decided to swallow all of the pills quickly. Soon, I felt good, except for the cold. The pills were hard to swallow, and I gagged, but I was almost there.

I felt my heart racing and then suddenly it seemed to almost stop. I saw my life again through the eyes of others, starting with my only son. Through his eyes, I was this beautiful strong queen who had shriveled into this weak cowardly peasant. I was no longer moving through life as though I owned it; instead, I was racing through it and seeking death.

I didn't want to see myself that way, so I saw my life through Madou's eyes. He didn't get to see all the lows. I'd always pretended that I was alright with him. He made me happy and when I was with him life felt good. I saw myself through his eyes: smart and amazing, beautiful and sexy, and powerful and ambitious—but I was not a Muslim. I didn't understand the culture or its core values.

The room darkened. Someone had entered and turned the light off. Unsure of who this was, I saw a small figure in the dark, a child who giggled. Who was this child running around in my bathroom? I heard her calling for my sister. She seemed to be playing hide and seek.

Noticing me lying in the bathtub, she came over to me. When I looked into her brown eyes, they were my own. This small child was me happy and free. I startled her as she startled me. She ran away and stopped at the door.

The room was now bright. *How did she reach the light switch?* The room radiated light, a yellow-purplish tint. I heard myself giggle as the little me ran from the room. "Wait!" I called to her, but she was gone. It was dark again. My hands were now numbed. I couldn't feel my fingers and there was a ringing in my ears. Going out didn't feel so bad. My heart didn't ache, and that shallow feeling that I'd had during the duration of my marriage was completely gone.

The small child entered the bathroom again with an adult. The figure was big with broad shoulders, and as she spoke to the child, I knew exactly who she was. She looked down at the small figure and grabbed her right hand. The child looked up intently. Her voice was just as sweet but stern as I remembered it as a child.

The woman spoke, "Geneva, what are you doing here in this bathroom? Did I not teach you better than this? Do you not remember everything that I told you? I never said life would be easy baby, but in order to get to the good, you're going to have to survive the bad. I could've quit, too, but I didn't because I had to live for you and your sister. My life was not perfect, Geneva. It was tough, and it was hard. I did not mean to deceive you into thinking that life was perfect. I did all that I could to create that illusion for you, child. Now you're here in this bathroom messing up your chance to get it right. People are always going to be people, they are going to judge you and talk about you, but you can't let them dictate your life. You cannot worry about what anyone else thinks, not even me. I am not perfect, Geneva. I can't raise your children. They need you and not me! I need you to fight for your life, girl!"

The child started to sob. My mother turned her around and walked out of the door. I wanted to cry out to my mom, but my tongue was too heavy, and my mouth seemed to be frozen shut.

She held the child's hand very tightly, almost squeezing it off. I remember when I'd be out shopping with her as a small child and when I did something that she didn't like, she grabbed my small hand tightly and I knew that I had to act right.

As they turned the corner, the small child looked back at me, and her eyes said that she was sorry. She didn't want to be here in this cold bathroom. I couldn't breathe. I wasn't breathing. The voices were right this was so easy.

I wasn't sure if I was in heaven. People all around me wearing scrubs were in a panic. Medical equipment was everywhere. The respirator to my left was helping me breath. *Why are these people trying to help me breath? I should be long gone by now.*

I knew the thin blonde to my right. She was an intensive care unit nurse in the hospital where I worked. I met her in the cafeteria a few months ago and again at the gym. She has a cat named Ally, and she can't seem to meet a nice guy anywhere. She said that she's never had a serious relationship and she is already 30. I remember when we talked one evening at the gym, and she told me some of her stories. I thought about how at 30 I was married with three children. I was either fast or she was slow. I thought it was a little bit of both.

I'd seen the tall Asian doctor before, too. I remember commenting as we walked through the cafeteria one day how incredibly tall he was. Perhaps he was related to the NBA player Yao Ming or something. There he was standing over me and giving orders. He needed a dose of this and a dose of that. I heard him yell out, "She's not gonna make it today." I started to pray, "God, I do not want to die. I am sorry for interfering with your work. Please forgive me." I did not die on that day because I heard the voice of the Lord say, "You will live and not die."

Madou said that he was worried about me for some time and spent the last few months just watching me from afar. He said that he watched me walk the kids to the end of my street in the mornings, and some days he watched me as I left for work. He said that he wasn't sure why he was worried, but he noticed that a weight gain around my mid-section months before, and he thought that I was pregnant with his child. He had a gut feeling that I was, but he did not know how to approach me. He said that, if I was pregnant, he'd step in and be a wonderful father to our child. As for his new bride, she would have any other choice but to accept it.

He said that, on this morning, he waited across the street to see me as my children walked alone. He knew that I usually left the house for work at eight, so at eight thirty he started to worry. My car was parked in its usual assigned spot. He had to leave for work because he had a very important nine o'clock meeting.

When he got to his company's parking garage, he looked down at his key chain and remembered that he had not returned the spare key that I'd given to him after our first year of dating. I told him that he could let himself in when the kids were away and wait on me to get home. He planned on going back to the apartment to check on me during his lunch break, but something told him to use the key if my car had not been moved.

Later he said that when he walked in, things looked normal and he immediately headed for my bedroom. He called out for me, "Geneva, Geneva, it's Madou! Are you home?' When he first saw my body, he knew that I was gone. My lips were blue, and I was so cold to touch. He quickly dialed 911 and waited for the ambulance to arrive and tell him that I was gone. While waiting, he said a prayer to God to save my life.

When the paramedics arrived, one of them yelled, "No pulse!" He knew that the woman he loved was gone. In that moment, he wished that he had gone against tradition and followed his heart. The second EMT entered the room and switched places with the first one. She got down next to my lifeless body and yelled, "I got a pulse! Let's go!"

I really didn't understand Madou's explanation of the events leading up to me being here at my job as a patient in the ICU. I knew that God was working out the details to save my life. I had never seen Madou watching me at any time. I'm usually very observant, but lately I was walking around in a fog and just feeling sorry for myself.

Madou stayed at the hospital until very late. He called my parents and gave the staff their number as my emergency contact. I didn't have any other family members in Boston, so the doctor called my parents and explained to them the severity of my condition. He said that I'd come very close to ending my life. In fact, if Madou had decided to wait until after work to come by and check in on me, I would've been dead for sure.

At that moment, I wasn't sure if I wanted to thank him or curse him. I now had to face life again and to live without my perfect life. My parents were flying in on Monday. Madou was kind enough to book and pay for their flights. I wasn't sure how I was going to face my parents or my children. I know that my parents didn't tell James what had happened, but I know that he was worried about me.

Because my parents would never want to cause hurt or pain to him, I imagined that they told him that perhaps I'd had an allergic reaction to some medicine.

My dad didn't condone lying and was known to always tell the truth. I envisioned him looking away and dropping his head as he told my only son that my actual suicide attempt was an accident. James was smart, and I know that he could sense that something else was going on. Most likely, my mom stepped in and assured him that I was okay.

After three days in the intensive care unit, I was informed by the doctor that I would be moving up to the ninth floor, which housed the psychiatric unit at the Brigham and Women's Hospital. I had worked here for almost eight years, and I knew almost all the staff from housekeeping to medical doctors. I had passed through to the cafeteria and exchanged my learned Spanish with some of the housekeeping staff. "Hola. Como Estas?" Some of my favorite people worked in the cafeteria and housekeeping.

I enjoyed many lunch conversations with a young ambitious Haitian gentleman. Pierre had migrated to Boston in the late nineties with his young wife and four children. His wife had taken to the fast crowd in Boston and was neglecting the family. He had worked there in housekeeping for the past 12 years and sometimes worked 16 hours a day to afford his family's first home. I thought about my last conversation with Pierre when he commented that he looked up to me. He said that he'd wished that his wife was more like me. If only Pierre could see me now….

My parents arrived on Monday as planned. I felt so ashamed, and I needed to cleanse my soul. I needed to tell my parents the truth as I couldn't stand to disappoint them.

My mom entered the room first and, of course, she was yelling, "Geneva! What's really going on with you? What were you thinking? I can't believe this; it makes no sense!" She didn't give me time to answer and just kept yelling.

My dad walked in slowly behind her. He didn't say a word and kept his eyes away from mine. I wanted him to come over and give me a hug. He'd been the only man who truly loved me, and I wanted to be in his arms.

I started to cry, and my mom calmed down and walked over to the side of the bed. She started to cradle me like I was a baby. I felt like a kid again in her arms. My dad sat in the only chair in the room, and he kept his eyes on the floor. I tried to speak with a knot in my throat that made it impossible to get out a word. I whispered as best I could, "I'm sorry." The very last thing that I wanted to do was to hurt my parents. I had already done so once by ending the vow that they believed to be sacred. Now here I was again, giving up. My mom had taught me to fight. I had to fight for anything that I really wanted. But what did I really want? I dozed off in my mother's arms. Before I closed my eyes, I looked over at my dad and I saw the tears dropping from his eyes. I saw the teardrops hitting the ceramic tile of the hospital floor, and I noticed that my dad didn't have any shoelaces in his sneakers. Sleep came upon me so peacefully, it reminded me of death.

I woke up a few hours later to find my parents still sitting and watching me. A nurse entered the room and was going over the treatment plan for me. I would be here for a few more days, and I'd be evaluated every four hours by the staff psychiatrists. When they felt like I was ready, they would release me for possible inpatient or outpatient treatment. I'd never seen this nurse before in the hospital, but she was kind. Her name was Denise, and her accent told me that she was possibly Irish but was born and raised in Boston. She told my dad that he could get his shoelaces from the checkout desk. It didn't dawn on me that they'd taken my dad's shoelaces because I could've used them to hurt myself.

The psychiatrist, Dr. Suarez, entered the room and introduced himself to us. Denise took my vitals as he walked around to my side of the bed. He started asking about my family history. They hadn't found any other drugs in my system other than the pills that I'd taken. He still asked if I'd used drugs or drank alcohol. My parents seemed to sit up and listen to see if there was something that they would learn about me through his questioning. I gave him permission to talk in front of my parents, and I designated my mother as my health care proxy so that she could make medical decisions for me if I couldn't do so on my own. Dr. Suarez was compassionate but stern. He asked about mental health issues in my family. I wasn't aware of anyone in my family who had suffered any mental breakdowns or schizophrenia or anything like that.

After all the questions, he advised that I should start on anti-depressants Lamictal and Klonopin. He said a therapist would visit twice a day. He gave me my first dose of pills and left. Denise asked my parents if they needed anything before she left. She also reminded them that visitation hours ended at eight o'clock. My mom asked if they could order something to eat. Denise said that they could go to the cafeteria and get food, but if they brought food back to the room, they had to stop at checkout for a list of items that they couldn't bring back, which included things like knives. My mom said that she would go down since my dad's shoes were too loose without his shoelaces.

As soon as my mom left, my dad got up and came closer to the bed. This was the first time that he'd looked directly at me. He looked into my eyes almost as though he was looking through me, and he was. He started to talk to the little girl deep down in there. There was always something magical about the way my dad seemed to take me back in time. He was so quiet, but when he talked, he talked to your spirit. His words echoed through the room as he sat down on the end of my bed. "Geneva, you know that you're better than all of this. You have your children to live for. Why would you end your life over a man? Do you think that your mom and I can raise all three of your kids? He waited for my answer. "No, dad." He scooted up closer to me, "Alright then, get yourself together. A man will come and go, but there's only one who will stay with you until the end of time, and I need you to find him, seek him, ask him for forgiveness and move on. The race is not won by the swift, but the one that endures, and, Geneva, you must endure. I've endured in this world with an eighth-grade education. I've endured some of the darkest days, baby girl, and I had to because of you and your sisters."

When my dad was really reflecting, he'd always include my oldest sister, Latoya. Sometimes, I'd forget that I wasn't his firstborn, but his firstborn with my mom. He always said that he wished he'd done better by Latoya, but when her mom moved, he had no way to reach her in Atlanta. I talked to Latoya every week. We'd been closer since I moved to Boston. I didn't want her to know my situation because I always seemed to have it all together. I gave her advice on men and money all the time. My dad spoke again, "We didn't tell your son what really happened, but, Geneva, he needs you more than anyone. He still doesn't understand why his dad is not in his life, and he's blaming you for that. Get yourself out of here and get back to him, and your daughters."

My parents left that night for the hotel. They had already called my kids' grandmother and told her about the "allergic drug reaction" that I'd had over the weekend. The girls wanted to come see me, but my mom didn't think it was a good idea, so she told them that I was having some weird side effects and would be home in a few more days. She preferred that the kids not see me this way. My ex-mother-in-law Shirley had no reasons not to believe my parents. I had become a pro at pretending, so no one who knew me would believe that I'd tried ending my life.

Even on my darkest days, I could put myself together and fake my way through the day. I'm not sure when I became such a good liar, but I had perfected the lie of being perfect. And I knew that in order to get out of here, I'd have to convince these trained psychiatrists and therapists that I was perfectly fine. I did a great job and was told on Tuesday that I'd be discharged home.

Had I gone crazy? No, I was simply at a point where I didn't think that I should live. It seemed like falling into a sleep forever was better than having to face the fact that my life was a mess. At that moment, the words of my father penetrated my heart. Seek God!

I returned home and took the rest of the week off from work. My director knew that I'd been admitted into the hospital, and I'm sure he heard some of the details. He left me a voicemail to call him if I needed more time off. No, as I'd already decided that I'd be back at work on the following Monday. My parents were spending the rest of the week with me and met me at the hospital with their luggage.

We caught a cab home, and the girls were there waiting for me. The day was a teachers' workday, so they were off from school. They had cleaned the house and the hardwood floors were shining and the place smelled of lilacs. They wanted me to feel better, and I must admit that as soon as I walked through the door I did. I began to look over my life, and for a few minutes, I didn't see all that I didn't have but only saw all that I had been blessed with. You see when you dwell on all the things that you don't have, life becomes bleak, especially when you compare your life with the lives of others. When I compared my life to my parents, well there was no real comparison and my life seemed short. But when I sat there on my living room couch on that day and thought about all my blessings, they surely outweighed those things that I didn't have. I had both parents, and they were available for me at any time. I have a tall, handsome, athletic son who would surely break barriers and change the world. My daughters were the most beautiful, smart, and caring girls that I'd ever met. And I was just given a second chance at life. My blessings were more than I could have asked for. In that moment of thought, my life was perfect.

7

The Search

I found myself seeking God daily for the next few weeks. I woke early each morning to sit in silent meditation before the kids were up. I opened my Bible for the first time in a very long time. I remember the first time I randomly opened it; it fell open to Isaiah 41:10: "So do not fear, for I am with you; do not be dismayed, for I am your God. I will strengthen you and help you; I will uphold you with my righteous right hand." I read that scripture over and over until it manifested in my spirit. I would no longer fear the thoughts of others, the idea of being alone, or being without a man. I would not fear anything in this life because my God is with me now. I had seen him on the morning that I'd tried to end my life. I'd seen him in the eyes of the small child that entered the bathroom. She looked like me, and I'm convinced that she was me, but her eyes were not my own. They belonged to the one who had created me in his very own image.

The next few months went by so fast; I really didn't have a whole lot of time to grieve the losses in my life. I spent all my time focusing on the wins. My son was excelling back in South Carolina, and my daughters were both doing well in school and were still very active. I was also doing very well in school. It seemed like when I first started looking for a graduate program, I found so many excuses why I couldn't do it. But I found the perfect place near the heart of Central Square. Cambridge College would be the place where I'd put all my extra energy outside of the word of God. I enrolled in the healthcare management program and promised myself that I would not only graduate but also graduate with honors.

Cambridge College was just what I needed during this time. My professors became close friends, and each classroom was like a small family. We all cared about each other academically and in life. The school was very diverse, too, as some of my new family/classmates came from places like Turkey, Ghana, Thailand, Singapore, Korea, Morocco, Nigeria, Costa Rica, and so many other places. I learned so much about the different cultures of the world that I felt like a world traveler though I hadn't left the United States.

In one of my finance classes on Saturdays, I noticed this dreary look in the face of one of my classmates. She was a very beautiful young lady, maybe in her early twenties, and her English was very broken, but she always seemed determined to learn. I asked if she was okay, and she said yes, but during class we made eye contact, and I saw that spirit of suicide that says, "my life is not worth living." I came to learn that it's so easy to identify things in others that we have or have been a part of. I couldn't wait until the class was over, and as soon as she left her seat, I rushed out behind her.

When we got on the elevator, I asked her if she had time to get a cup of coffee with me. She obliged, and as we sat in that small cafe, two broken women from two different parts of the world and with totally different issues, we shared the same thought: "I don't want to live." I told her immediately that I'd tried to end my own life and that it's God's will that we live to make our impact on the world. She began to weep. I cried as I shared with her my testimony. It was so easy telling it freely without the lies. It was easier to tell her because outside of class she was a stranger.

As we continued sharing, with both of us crying through thoughts and memories, the voice of God spoke to me. I spoke it to her as the words penetrated my heart. What is the worst thing in the world that could ever happen to you? I asked. She looked up confused at the question. I responded, "the worst thing that could happen to you is if God stops loving you, and since that could never happen, it means that the worst thing that could ever happen to you will never happen, so why worry about all of the other stuff?" I thanked God for those words that he gave me to share with this beautiful young Nigerian woman who thought that her life was going to end.

We sat in the cafe for more than three hours, the sun was beginning to set, and I needed to get home to the girls because I had promised them an evening out. She thanked me for saving her life, and I thanked her for allowing me to be honest with her because I hadn't been honest with anyone about myself in a very long time.

On the way out, I reached in my bag and noticed that I missed eight calls all from my mom. I turned my ringer off in class and forgot to turn it back on. My mom was still worried and always wanted to know if I was still taking my anti-depressants. I always told her that I was, but I stopped taking them on the day that I left the hospital. I no longer feared losing my life again, as I had sought God and he was there with me every single minute of every hour of every day. I started working out after my morning meditation and my body started to sculpt into the one in which I owned when I was around 18 years old. I was no longer seeking validation from others. I didn't go to church at all; for me, it was just God, my children, school, and work.

I spent more time with God during the next few months than I had done my entire life and it was amazing and refreshing. You see in church I would have to fit into a mold that man had created. I'd have to pray when it was praying time and to sing when it was time for a hymn. I'd have to dress a certain way and sit a certain way. I'd have to pretend to fit into that mold. But with this alone time, I could humble myself unto the Lord at any time. There was no reason to pretend; no faking. It was just me and God. Sometimes I would cry out to him in praise and thanksgiving and at other times in pure anguish. I spent so many days face down on my living room floor just praying and seeking, praying and seeking. My daughters sometimes joined me because I'd taught them to pray at an early age.

My mom had taught us to say our prayers by the time we could talk. I still called my son often to remind him to say his prayers. Being with God was easy; in fact, I learned over the course of the first few months out of the hospital that it's so easy to be with God because he is always with me.

*****

I desperately needed to see my only son, so I planned another weekend trip to South Carolina to visit him. I enjoyed sharing my old room with him. He had gotten so tall and his voice was getting deep. The last time I'd called my parents' house, I thought that he was my dad. I was proud of him because he was doing well, even after all that he'd been through with the divorce from his dad and the feelings of abandonment after I made the decision to send him south. And I did say, "the divorce from his dad." I learned that many times when parents get divorced, the non-custodial parent divorces the kids, too. His dad had not taken a stand for him. He didn't offer to take him when I was finding it difficult to be a mother and a father to a growing teenage boy. But my son moved past all that, and I was so proud. He was determined to do the right things, to be a good man, and to be there for his sisters and mom. I didn't want him to take that position. It was not his job to take care of me or his sisters, but I felt honored and humbled because my son would one day grow up to be the second man to ever love me. I was beginning to see how perfect life really could be without the false perceptions.

The weekend in South Carolina went by so fast. I spent Friday night watching my son's team play basketball. My God how tall he had gotten in a few short months. He was nearly six feet tall and only 15 years old. They didn't win that night, but he played hard. We rode back to my parents' house, and he shared with me all the new and exciting things that were happening in his life. He told me his plans and aspirations for the future. He said that there was only one thing more that he wanted in life and that was to be with his sisters and me. I cried and made him a promise, "As soon as I graduate from college, your sisters and I will be here." I saw the excitement in his eyes as his face lit up. When I told my parents, both were ecstatic, especially my mom. She didn't like the idea of me living in the big city of Boston without any family. I told her that I had friends who were just like family, and my city was safer than most. My son and I went to church with my parents. I wish that I'd brought the girls, despite the expensive flights (mine was $425). They understood and didn't complain about going to spend some time with their grandmother. Church was good, I hadn't been in a long time, and it was nice.

My son and I prayed together before I left for my flight back to the city. I held him in my arms in awe that my little boy was now hovering over me. I saw tears forming in his eyes and he dropped his head so that I could not see him cry. I kissed him and told him I loved him more than anything else in the world. I thanked God for my ex-husband on that day for the very first time since our divorce. I thanked God that he had given me this handsome perfect boy. I thought, *I'll be back after I graduate, son.*

Graduation was just four months away. I'd been so busy trying to get rid of things that I surely wasn't taking with me to South Carolina. I told my friends that it was official: moving back to South Carolina in July. My grades were exemplary, and my relationship with God was blossoming. My daughters and used Skype with my son every other night to tell him about what we were doing in preparation for the move. The girls were as excited as their brother. I could tell that they all just wanted to be together. I had raised them that way, and I couldn't change the past. I could only make the future as great for them possible.

My parents and son were now planning a trip to Boston for my graduation. This would be their first real trip here, so I wanted to make it fun for them. Their actual first trip was spent by my side in a hospital room. I was so excited for them to see how much better I was doing, and that it wasn't a lie. I was living in my truth. Everything was the way that it was supposed to be without any misperceptions.

Life was moving by so fast. My friends were planning a going-away party for me on the following week. I wasn't looking forward to it at all because saying goodbye to them was going to be one of the hardest things for me to do. I had grown to love this group of people with whom I initially had nothing in common just as much as I loved my own family. They had stood by me through the thick and the thin. I don't understand why it was so hard for me to be honest with them. I knew that they all loved me unconditionally. Lennett was planning the party. I was a little leery about her doing the planning because she had such exquisite taste. I told her that I didn't want an extravagant event, just something nice and simple. Lennett was Caribbean-American, tall, and walked as though she was a part of the royal family of England. Though she was extremely beautiful, once I got to know her, she was one of the humblest persons I'd ever met. I'd met her at the hospital where I worked part-time. Lennett was honest and caring, and she told me often how much she admired me. I called on her whenever I needed to have my spirits lifted. She never judged me and always told me something that left me smiling. She once told me that she thought that Madou would be my husband and she saw me having another child. I was never sure about either, but it sounded good.

I also had a few of my professors who I'd wanted to invite. I was fond of all of them, but my English professor was amazing. I guessed that we were around the same age, and when I met her, I was immediately drawn to her knowledge. I'd taken all her classes, even as electives if I didn't need them. Professor Gina is what we all called her, and she was so attentive to her students. We talked often after class, and she looked over the commencement speech I would be giving in just a couple more weeks. I gave Lennett Gina's contact information and told her to make sure that she invited her.

I also reached out to all my former students who I'd coached in basketball. I asked them to come along with their parents. Also invited were all of my children's former teachers and principals who were all a vital part of my life.

I even reached out to my aunt who lived in New York. Shortly after my divorce, I drove to New York and spent a weekend or two with my mother's sister. She visited me in Boston on a few occasions, and each time she visited she left with the same words, "I'm proud and amazed at how perfect your life is. You and Gregory have done what a lot of young couples have not done, and you've made it work."

I wanted to tell her on one occasion that I made it work because I lived a lie. I wanted to tell her that I am married to a man who will never be faithful to me, and I'm just as unfaithful to him. But, of course, I smiled and replied, "Thank you, auntie."

Thanks to all my friends, the party was amazing. We had a DJ who played the best music, and we danced and laughed the night away. My aunt brought my cousins up from New York, and almost everyone who'd touched my life in any kind of way was there. I was sitting at one of the tables talking to a professor about graduation, when out of the corner of my eye, I saw him standing there. It had been so long, and I wondered who had invited him? Lennett had asked me if she could invite him and I said no. I had not explained the events that led up to our breakup, not because I was trying to lie, I just didn't want to relive it each time I spoke about it. I knew that she wouldn't have invited him. But what I didn't realize was that Madou and I still shared some of the same friends, and a few of them had been invited. I found out later that a mutual friend from the gym had mentioned to him that she was coming. She didn't know that we were not together anymore. And yet here he was, standing there and he looked so handsome.

My first instinct was to run over to him and let him wrap his huge arms around me and tell me how safe I am again. But my spirit woman spoke, and to do so would be totally against all that I'd work to become. I didn't want to ever be that woman who would have a secret rendezvous with another woman's husband knowing that he was going home to his wife and children. I wanted to live freely and in the will of God. I made a promise on that night that I would have to dig deeper than my feelings and do what's right. Feelings are just emotions that can die down if you command them to, and because I now owned my life, I would speak to all the things in my life and have them move.

Feelings of lust, step aside, I commanded as I walked over to him. "Hi, Madou. How have you been? What brings you here tonight?" He didn't answer right away, and then he smiled. It was an honest smile. He replied, "I just wanted to say goodbye." He reached in as if to give me a hug and I moved closer to him and we embraced. The embrace was filled with love and respect. I knew that Madou felt the same way. He didn't want to sin against his marriage or cause me any harm. He simply wanted to say goodbye. I appreciated the "good" in goodbye on that night, and I understood that not all things and people are meant to be in your life forever.

I thanked God for Madou's life and the good times that we shared. I didn't dwell on the things that went wrong. Tears began to fall, and I rushed into the bathroom because I knew that a few of my friends were watching. I came back into the reception hall, and the DJ was now playing some salsa. I hit the dance floor quickly and let the tears flow. Before I knew it, all my friends had gathered around, and I was now in a tight circle of love.

The music stopped, and for the first time in a very long time, I realized that I was free from the bondage of pretending to be who someone else thought that I should be. I was free to not be my mother. I was free from not being perfect. Yes, I was crying uncontrollably now—all happy tears. I was in love again for the first time since I was a teenager. I was in love with Geneva Wallace Grant, and I was grateful for all the love that I shared with these beautiful people whom God had placed in my life for this very moment. I was grateful for this circle to be formed around me and filled with so much love.

8

The Accomplishment

My parents were coming here for graduation in just two days. In preparation, I spent the weekend cleaning and packing. The only thing left in my apartment were the big things: sofa, beds, and dressers, which I decided to give to a nearby boarding house for women. They would pick them up the day before I left for South Carolina. I've been excited for days to see my parents and my son again. My daughters were finishing up the last few weeks of school, while my son finished over a week ago. The girls complained that school started too soon in South Carolina and because they were getting out later in Boston, their summer vacation would be shorter.

Every time they started complaining, I reminded them about how nice it will be to all be in South Carolina. I was moving into a family house that I'd purchased when I was married and had spent a few years fixing it up. It was fully furnished. My ex-husband and I had planned to move there once all the kids had left the house for college. The small modern home sat on almost two acres of land, and our plan was to include an in-ground pool, garden, and a basketball hoop out back—southern living at its finest.

Now, I was grateful that I could occupy this house with my three children. They would enjoy the old dirt roads that I'd played on as a kid, without a care in the world, except the streetlight. Coming home after the streetlight meant one of a few things: dinner was already over and you were going to bed hungry, mom had a switch in her right hand, or both. I'd give anything to go back to those days when life was perfect, and we didn't have a care in the world.

Graduation practice was scheduled for six o'clock in the evening. I'd practiced my commencement speech so hard that the entire thing was now a part of my memory. I could recite it at any time and had done so on my walks to work for prior the month. My classmates and I had worked so hard for this day. It was not easy working full-time and completing an undergraduate and graduate degree. Cambridge College had made it easier for us, though, the structure of the classroom and the hand-on instruction along with life applications and professors who really cared about your success all made this place so perfect for me. I'm not sure if I would have received this kind of education anywhere else. The College was located just a few blocks from Harvard, but for me there was no comparison. I had taken an elective class at Harvard a few summers ago, and I wasn't very impressed after comparing it to my alma mater.

There was something magical about the evening of practice. It was a very warm evening, and there was a slight low-rising fog. I walked to Boston Harbor, and during the hour walk, I just thanked God that I had survived. I had lived through the very things that I had convinced myself would surely kill me. Aborting my unborn child haunted me the most. I couldn't seem to get past the fact that I had done such a thing. Something always kept telling me that it wasn't as bad because it was legal, but you know deep down in your soul that man's law doesn't justify God's truth.

I reached the rehearsal to find all my classmates hanging around waiting on instructions. These people were my third family after my dearest friends. I loved them all and not superficially. Throughout the years, we'd gotten to know each other, and although we were so diversified, we all shared one common thing. We all wanted more in life: more knowledge, more happiness, more understanding, and more love. "More" was the common denominator that linked us all together.

In the right-hand corner was Jessie, a Boston native whose passion was to someday open her own restaurant. For the past couple of years, she cooked dinners for us and brought them to school. Of course, they were for sale, and it was the best $10 I'd ever spent. Most of her food was Caribbean influenced. She was at the rehearsal with a few boxes of dinners, and I hadn't ordered one, but she usually brought extras.

It was only 5:30, so I walked over to see what she had cooked. As I approached her table, I smelled all the island aromas. I wasn't hungry, but that hour walk put me in the mood for some good jerk shrimp and, of course, she had an extra plate. Jessie had just gotten married, so I asked her about the wedding.

I admired her for her drive. She worked a full-time job and attended college full-time in the evenings and yet still managed to find some time for her passion for cooking. I didn't discuss much of my personal drama with my classmates. However, when Jessie asked how my husband was doing, I thought, *This is the perfect opportunity to tell the truth about my life for once.* I looked her straight in the eyes, and I said "I've been divorced for over a year. My ex-husband still lives here, but I don't see him very often." Jessie almost choked on my words.

When Jessie and I first met, I talked about my life in the same way that I wanted people to see it. I maintained the illusion that things were perfect when, in fact, they were far from it. I did not mention my husband's infidelity because I was not a saint. Finally, I had reached a place in my life where I was no longer going to make excuses or spread blame.

I made the choice to ignore the first time my husband was unfaithful. Later, I alone made the decision to stay with him, as we created an unspoken pact that we would both see other people if it did not impose on our perfect family. These were my decisions and mine alone, and the days of blaming him or anyone else were over.

I ate my jerk shrimp and talked with Jessie until it was time to get in line for rehearsals. I learned on that night that I wouldn't be marching in with my classmates; instead I'd be coming in with the faculty. I thought that I would lead my classmates into the graduation and then walk up to the stage when it was my turn to give the commencement speech. I was totally thinking back to my high school graduation.

I had just turned 18, and my baby was moving around in my stomach as though she was skipping rope. South Carolina is hot in June, and we were lined up outside the graduation venue. My best friend, Monique, kept checking to see if I was doing okay. I was tired, and I was sad. My classmates were all talking about college or the military, and a few others were going to work in their family's businesses. They were all excited about the years ahead.

I wondered what Gregory was doing. I heard that he was seeing a girl who went to one of the nearby colleges. One day in the cafeteria, a girl from my high school who I didn't even talk to sharply asked, "I saw Gregory dropping you off the other day. Did you know he's dating my cousin at USC?"

I wanted to throw up because this was during my first trimester, and I had hidden the pregnancy from everyone. I didn't reply to her question and ran out of the cafeteria to the bathroom to vomit. She thought that I ran away just crying, but I cried later that night at home. I wouldn't dare let some high school freshman see me cry over a man, and surely not over the man I thought would be with me forever.

I asked Gregory about it that evening and, of course, he said that it was not true. The girl in question was someone he'd dated before he even met me, and her cousin was surely just trying to break us up.

That would be Gregory's usual answer for almost all of his affairs. A few days later, this same girl came up to me again and said that Gregory was driving her cousin's mom to her college graduation, which was the same day as mine. I decided to not bother Gregory again with these accusations, and I told him that I wanted him to be at my graduation. He said that he wouldn't miss it for the world. He said that me and our unborn daughter meant everything to him.

As I stood in my high school graduation practice line, I realized that I hadn't heard from Gregory all day. I tried to call him and only got voicemail. I didn't hear from Gregory for the next three days. He didn't attend my graduation, and I knew where he'd been.

I took that walk across the stage to get my high school diploma, and it felt more like "the walk of shame." I didn't dare look over at my parents because I sensed their disappointment. They were proud that I earned my diploma and disappointed that I was a single teenage mom. If Gregory had come, he would have shown my parents that he was already standing beside me and that life was not over for me. Just a few months later, Gregory and I were married.

*****

Graduation practice was quick. I mean we were mostly adults who had conquered many of life's challenges, and so we could surely follow marching instructions. I would be sitting next to my dean, Mr. Sutton, who had become more than a dean. He was a confidant, the first and only person who I told that I was pregnant. I was late for my Thursday evening class on many occasions, and my professor had casually mentioned this to the dean who caught me getting on the elevator one day and asked if I had a few minutes.

When we entered his office, he quickly began asking, "So you're never late for class and you've now been late every evening for the last month. Is there anything that I can do?"

I softly smiled and told him that I was pregnant. A huge smile darted across his face, and he congratulated me, and then said that he understood. "Just let Professor Q know so he can work with you."

Professor Q was a stickler for time. He taught Human Resources and thought that every minute counted because there was so much that he wanted us to learn. I didn't go to Professor Q and tell him anything, I just got to class on time, even about 15 minutes early on Thursdays.

Mr. Sutton never asked me again about my pregnancy as it was evident that I was no longer pregnant. The halter shirt that I was wearing showed the silhouette of my flat belly. I had taken my sweatshirt off after an hour-long walk and tied it around my waist.

*****

Mr. Sutton went to the podium and practiced my introduction, and I got up and said just the first few lines of my speech as we flowed through the practice. After practice, we all gathered together to chat just a little while before making our way to the parking lot. It was now dark outside, and a few of my classmates asked if I needed a ride. I loved walking in Cambridge, and even though it was dark, I felt completely safe. I walked home that evening, still thankful for this second chance. I was about to do something that no one in my immediate family had ever done. I thanked God for the privilege. I thanked God that I had not lost my mind and, most importantly, I did not die.

*****

My parents and my son had a flight delay. I'd planned on picking them up at eight o'clock in the morning and then heading into work. As they wouldn't arrive until noon, my girlfriend Myeisha agreed to pick them up. She was off on Fridays now and initially volunteered to get them. I really wanted to be there when they got in because I missed my son. I couldn't wait to hug him. He was exceptionally tall and his shoulders had begun to broaden. For some reason, I now felt safe when I hugged him.

But I was off to work, and Myeisha took care of my parents and son. She got them settled in at the house and made sure they had everything that they needed while I was at work and my daughters were in school.

On the phone on an earlier day, my son was bragging to his sisters that he'd been out of school for almost a month while they're still going. Cambridge had some snow days to make up and school lasted until mid-June. My son didn't realize that he started school in South Carolina in August, and school in Boston didn't start until after Labor Day—almost net even.

When I got home, mom and dad were sitting in the living room watching Jeopardy. Mom said the kids had gone out to meet friends at the school park. Dad had a worried look on his face, but didn't say much. I hoped that they were not still worrying about me. I'd done a good job at getting back on track since that last incident. Most importantly, I was no longer pretending to be anyone that I wasn't.

Things weren't easy for me, but I was doing all that I could do to make things better. I didn't see a therapist that often, and still knew that if I needed to, I could schedule an appointment without hesitation. I didn't like the nervous look my dad gave me, as he looked concerned.

The previous time that they'd seen me, I was lying in a bed in the psychiatric unit of the hospital in which I'd worked for the last 10 years. I was weak and confused and unsure about living. I made a vow to God that I'd never go back to that sick state again, and I hoped that my parents knew that, too.

I headed into the kitchen to start dinner. My mom got up behind me, leaving my dad on the sofa.

"Geneva, you look good."

"Thanks, mom, I'm feeling really good these days."

My mom went on the explain how worried I had made them and that she knew that I knew better than to do that. She told me that she and dad were still proud of me. She asked about the medications and therapy. I told her that I was no longer on the meds, but that I now meditated and prayed about difficult thoughts.

We continued to prepare dinner and talk. My mom asked me questions loud enough for my dad to hear. I imagined his ears were locked to the other side of the thin wall because he needed to hear my answers for himself. He needed to know that I was okay.

And for the first time in a very long time, I really was all right. I had no desire to be anyone other than who I was in this very moment. I was love and light. I'd survived what I thought were the darkest times of my life. I was convinced that my past would stay there and wither up and die.

I texted my son and told him to head home for dinner. It felt like old times when I'd have to call him in from the nearby basketball court. We'd always sit together and have dinner, and now it was nice having my parents there with us. Of course, James replied, "Can Carlos come over for dinner, Ma?" I replied yes, and it felt so good. I always cooked more than enough because the kids always brought friends over for dinner.

When I was young, my mom always said, "Don't bring other kids over for dinner, as we don't have enough to feed extra people." I always thought it an honor and privilege to cook for all the kids.

I remember the kids having six friends over once when we lived in Harvard Square. I'd made pasta that evening with eggplant. I didn't eat dinner that night because I'd barely had enough for all the kids. That's what started me on always cooking more than enough so we could feed the sweaty teenage boys who followed James home, knowing that his mom would fill their bellies.

We all sat down to eat dinner. I grabbed the extra chair from my bedroom for Carlos. I made eggplant parmesan and added chicken for my parents. I made a huge Greek salad, and my famous homemade dressing made from a co-worker's recipe.

James talked about school in South Carolina and how easy it was compared to Cambridge. My dad talked about how much James's basketball skills had improved. I loved talking basketball with my dad. He taught me how to play, and I taught my only son and daughters. The girls said that they were excited to be moving down south. They always enjoyed their summers there, and they loved my mom's southern cooking. We talked about all the things that we were going to do once we got to South Carolina. My son said that he couldn't wait to drive because everything was so far, and there was no public transportation. That reminded me that I would really miss hopping on a bus or train to get to the mall or downtown where the traffic was too congested to drive.

We enjoyed dessert after dinner: fruit pie and some ice cream picked up on the way home from work. We weren't big on desserts, but always had one for a special occasion. Tonight, was a special occasion. I had my family all together at my dinner table, and I was free to be myself. Graduation was at 11 o'clock in the morning, and I had to be there at 9:30, meaning my friends would pick up my parents and the kids around 10.

*****

Graduation day was magical, leaving me without words to describe the excitement that I felt in my heart. When I received my undergraduate degree, it wasn't much of a big deal. I chose not to march with my class because it had been such a difficult time in my life. Pretending to have a perfect life wasn't always easy, and during the end of my last year in my undergraduate program, things were getting bad inside my house. Sure, we still did a good job for the world to see, but my husband at that time seemed to be taking on new lovers like crazy. I assumed it was right before he met the mother of his child because he came home with different scents. Perhaps his lover was wearing different types of perfume? No, this was not the case. Sometimes, I would investigate just to find out who I was sharing my husband with. I always had access to our cell phone records, and he never thought of me as a snooper. I guess he knew that I really didn't want to know about all his affairs. I'd shown him early on that I could easily close my eyes and keep it moving.

But during this time, he was hardly talking to me, and our love making was the worst. If he touched me once a month, I was lucky. I wanted to see who was getting all of his wife's loving. The phone records revealed that he was now dating a biracial twin from Portsmouth, New Hampshire. Her mother was Irish, and her dad was Jamaican.

From the transcripts of the texts, they met in a bar in Harvard Square. She was pleasantly plump with fiery red hair. Her name was Nicole. She was 30, which made her a little old for my husband's liking, but she seemed playful. She smoked weed and drank heavily. I envisioned my husband's hands in her curly red locks as she puffed on some exotic Jamaican weed. She caught the train into Boston on Thursday afternoons and met him usually near downtown. She paid for a hotel room and stayed there until Sunday. She knew that he was married, and he told her the same story, "I'm only with my wife because of my three kids. I'm planning to leave her soon."

I often wondered how women believed such foolery. But it had always worked for him, and I realized that people believe what they want to believe. But silly Nicole, my husband was also telling those same lies to another young woman who he met in Dorchester at his cousin's house.

This new young woman, Ebony, was in the right age bracket for my 40-year-old husband. She was 24 and the single mother of two small children. The children's father was imprisoned for drug-related charges. She was tall and thin and extremely beautiful.

Ebony was a little rough around the edges after growing up on the rough streets of Roxbury. Her mom was addicted to drugs, and so Ebony raised herself. She had gotten pregnant at 19 by an older man, and, at 22, she met her youngest daughter's father. He was an aspiring rapper and local drug dealer, and he provided for her and her children. She didn't have to work because he took care of her.

Poor Ebony, I knew right away that my husband would fill this void of her not having a father. I read her texts to and from my husband, and on one night when he was supposed to meet Nicole, Ebony demanded to see him. She said that she was tired of all of this, "I'm leaving my wife as soon as I get things straight with my kids." She said that my husband made her give up all her friends so all she did was wait on him.

I wanted to call Ebony and give her some advice because I felt sorry for her, but I should have felt even sorrier for myself. I never confronted my husband about these women. I just let him continue to see them. I kept my perfect family together while I suffered inside. And besides, I'd just met a young man who seemed to know how to make all my worries disappear.

That year had been a tough year for me indeed. I received my bachelor's degree in healthcare management and didn't care about walking across the stage. Yet here I was about to walk across the stage after addressing my faculty, peers, family, and friends in a commencement speech that I'd written just a few weeks before.

I'll never forget the look on my parents' or children's faces. I could see that they were so very proud of me for receiving my master's degree and in overcoming life's challenges. I looked behind my parents and children and saw all my friends from Boston. These people were my family. I was honored to have my auntie and her daughter from New York there. It was a blessing.

I learned on that day that anything is possible. I had just experienced the worst time of my life: lost my marriage, family, and mind just a year ago. Now, here I was standing before all the people who I loved as a survivor. I was now more than a conqueror because I'd not only taken control of my life but had also rid myself of a lie that I'd lived for more than half of my existence. Though it was too embarrassing to tell my entire truth, I was no longer living a lie.

9

Confronting the Truth

⸻ ❦ ⸻

After graduation, we all headed back to my place in Cambridge. Graduation had been outside on the Boston Harbor, and it was the most beautiful June day I'd ever seen. The sun was bright, and the humidity was low. A subtle wind blew, blessing us with just enough relief from the sun's heat. My parents and my kids all hopped in my car. My dad sat crammed in the back seat with the kids.

I told my friends that I'd meet them at my house. Myeisha had a key, so she got there first to let them in, as I needed to pick up a few things from the Whole Foods Market. I loved to shop there though I didn't go very often because it was near my ex-husband's new apartment. But that was now my past, and I was free to go wherever I wanted to go. In a few short weeks, I would be back in South Carolina. I knew exactly what I needed, so I parked close and told the gang that I'd be out in a few short minutes.

My kids would love the cheesecake that I ordered, and the fresh fruit and veggie tray for everyone at the house to snack on while I finished preparing dinner. I also needed seltzer water, mixed nuts, and cheese and crackers. In less than 10 minutes, I'd gathered everything and headed to the register, when I thought to grab a bag of tortillas and dip. I expected about 30 people waiting back home, and I didn't want them to be hungry while waiting on my mom and I to finish cooking.

As soon as I turned the aisle with Mexican foods, there she was—my ex-husband's lover and young daughter. I wanted to turn around, but it was too late. This was the first time that I'd been this close to the child who'd ruined my family. I wanted to call her a bastard baby, but she was beautiful and had my ex-husband's eyes. I silently asked God to forgive me for my past discretions regarding this beautiful little baby. She looked to be of Asian, European, and African American descent.

I felt a wave a peace come upon me as I grabbed the bag of snacks. Just as I turned around, the mother walked directly toward me and was now summoning me to stop.

"Well hey there, old lady. Gregory told me that you called my child a bastard. Well, she is not a bastard, and she didn't do anything to you. Gregory left you because he said that you were no good, and I was the best thing that ever happened to him. He's now with me and our child and he will be with me forever."

I looked at her for maybe 30 seconds and replied quickly, "You remind me of me more than 15 years ago. I feel sorry for you because you know what you are and were not Gregory's only lover behind my back. I did the exact same thing by becoming pregnant with hopes that he'd only be with me and my child. Good luck with that, and God bless you and your daughter who was born out of wedlock of my marriage!"

I headed to the register to pay for my items, and I silently thanked God for this young woman. Had it not been for her, I would've still been imprisoned in that lie. Instead, I was walking out of the store free of the madness of knowingly sharing my husband with other women and feeling that I was not being enough to satisfy one man.

As I threw the bags in the trunk, I couldn't help but laugh out loud. This little girl has no idea of what forever is going be like with my ex-husband, Gregory. Good luck!

When we arrived back at my place, my friends had already loaded up on snacks and were ready to start a game of spades. My son quickly changed into his basketball clothes and sneakers as he waited for his neighborhood friends to come by. My oldest daughter helped in the kitchen as my youngest headed over to watch the spades game. Theresa was making drinks. She said that she'd make my favorite, "the Cape-Codder" that mixed vodka and cranberry. I still wasn't at ease having drinks around my parents, but my days of pretending were over.

I remembered years ago how I hid my drinking from them. I didn't want them to know that I drank alcohol. Strange, because I was 30-plus years old with three kids and my own house. It always mattered so much what my parents thought. I mean when I was young, my parents used to enjoy cocktails and beers. They'd drink and get merry and swing dance each other across the house. But in that perfect world that I'd conjured up in my mind, I wanted everything about to me be perfect, especially to my parents.

I grabbed my mixed drink from Theresa openly and enjoyed its flavor. We had one of the best times that evening in a long time. After a few drinks, I turned into a dancing machine. They call it liquid courage because I was a horrible dancer, but my friends all knew that after a few drinks, I would out dance the best dancers in the world, at least in my mind.

My dad whispered to me right before dinner, "I didn't know you were a vodka girl. I only drank brown liquor in my drinking days." I got nervous talking about drinking with my dad, and he wasn't disappointed or angry. In fact, he seemed excited and happy for me. I just prayed that my drinking friends didn't make too much of the scene, and they didn't because they'd heard me talk about my parents, and though they were themselves, there was no table dancing or removing of clothing.

I woke up the next morning with the worst headache and a house filled with leftover people. My parents were in my bedroom, so I opted to sleep in the girls' bedroom. That plan changed to me waking up on the living room floor with my son at my feet and my girlfriend and her fiancé on the couch. Myeisha and Grisel were both huddled up near the dining room table. I stumbled in to check on the girls and they had a room filled with friends. I remembered a couple of their friends had come by a with their parents whom I had been social with through coaching the girls. I didn't remember giving the okay for them to stay the night, but I'm sure that I did. I checked into James's room and it was empty. I imagined that he came out to the living room to watch TV or something and fell asleep on the floor with me.

I began to clean up the place a little while not making too much noise so as not to disturb everyone else. I had always been an early riser, no matter how much I drank or how long I stayed up I could never sleep past six o'clock. I decided to wash my face and take a walk. I loved early morning walks in Massachusetts. For a metropolitan city, the place had an ambiance of Cape Cod. I walked to the Charles River and decided to just sit out there and pray. I've always loved my alone time with God on the river or at the ocean. I find that nature is God's perfect creation more so than us. Nature never goes against the grain like we do. It does exactly what God instructs it to do, making everything around it flow perfectly. It doesn't have to pretend. What you see in nature is what you get. I prayed on the river, "God, please allow me to be more like your perfect creation."

My parents and my son were headed back to South Carolina in the morning. They were all packed and ready to go. I was ready to go also. I loved Boston and Cambridge so very much, but my soul desired to be in the south. I saw areas in which God could use me to bless the people there and change their lives for the best. I saw my purpose there, and I wasn't afraid. I'd been afraid my entire life, but right now I wasn't bound to anything. I was starting to resemble the ocean. I was just flowing.

I dropped my family off at the airport, and the girls and I finished getting ready for our big move. The women's shelter was coming to pick up all the furniture in the morning and I had already rented the U-Haul that I would attach to the car for the 1,000-mile drive to South Carolina. The girls and I planned a week-long driving vacation. We would stop in three states and spend the night after touring them. We decided on Maryland, Washington, and North Carolina. I booked the hotels in each state and checked out things to do as tourists.

For the rest of the week prior to our departure, I met with old friends and colleagues who hadn't made it to the going-away bash. We met for lunch, dinner, and sometimes just for a quick walk. We reminisced over many good days, and I felt relieved that many of them no longer commented on how perfect they thought my life was. They were no longer seeing me through the illusion that I'd created for so many years. They all knew parts of my story and the fact that I'd come near death by trying to end my own life, so I wasn't perfect, just struggling to find peace like everyone else. I desired to be more like nature and more like God.

We packed up and hit the road. I was starting a new chapter in my life, and I was nervous but not afraid. Our little excursions went great and stopping provided me with the rest that I needed. Driving the U-Haul to South Carolina was the first step in taking control of my life moving forward. I could've used a moving company perhaps, but we only had our clothes and precious items with us, including my daughter's hope chest that was given to her by her grandmother.

We arrived in South Carolina three days later, and to our surprise, my son was at the house alone waiting for us. He had been calling every few hours to see where we were and seemed just as anxious as his sisters. I had done all the spring cleaning to the house when I was here a few months earlier. It was hot in South Carolina, though, and we were thankful that James had turned on the air in our new family home. He helped us to unload the U-Haul. We laughed and talked. He told his sisters how much different the people were here. He said, "It's gonna take you guys some time to get used to them." They would have the entire summer to hang out and get to know their cousins.

The only thing that was difficult for us was living without public transportation. I had to drive them everywhere. I took money out of my 401K, as I didn't plan to work right away. I wanted to enjoy this summer with my children and move closer to God's purpose for me. I decided to take on a personal challenge of non-judgement. For the next month, I would try to live a life of non-judgement. I wouldn't judge anyone or anything. While practicing non-judgement, I could focus solely on myself. I needed to be my best so that I could be the best for my children. Yes, I had done a great job hiding a lot of my sorrows from them, but my children were not babies and instead were three of the most intellectual teenagers that I'd met. They were smart enough not to let me know that they knew more than I thought they did.

Our first night together in our new home was magical. We all laid around and listened to James's stories about South Carolina. He said that there was no diversity. I told him that was the case when I was a child. There were only two types of people "Black American" and "White American." The girls couldn't believe that it was still this way. My son told stories about kids from school who had tried dating outside of their race, and it almost started a race war. The girls didn't believe it, and I didn't believe it. I'd been gone for 15 years and surely things had changed a little. My kids knew very little about race tension. They had friends from all over the world: Turkey, Ireland, Saudi Arabia, Africa, Cape Verde, and Germany, just to name a few. And they liked people according to their spirits. It didn't matter what a person looked like, but how their spirits felt. This was probably going to be the biggest change for them, yet I knew that they would adapt. I had raised resilient kids. We started our family Bible study. I had grown leery of church gatherings and some of the falsehoods and rituals that the church practiced.

I learned that it was much easier to serve God in spirit and in truth when you were in truth and not in a room filled with people who are all pretending to be something that someone else thought they should be. I'd spent my entire adult life doing that, so I had no intentions of doing it in church.

We learned the scriptures at home, and learned how to practice them in our daily living. I taught my children all that God had shown me, and my son was always excited to learn more about the Lord.

After about two months of being at home, we decided to attend a church service with my dad. We visited the small church that I'd grown up in and, as expected, all things were the same. They sung the same hymns and did the same prayers that they did when I was a young girl. The only difference was they had a young innovative pastor, and he and his wife were a beautiful addition to the place. His sermons were great, and his knowledge of the word was intact. I could learn from him and so could my children. It was a good time, and I was shocked on the evening that my only son told me he wanted to give his life to the Lord. I was shocked because I'd thought my daughters would've been the first to do so. At 15 years old, I didn't think my son would have been the first. But I was grateful because growing up in Cambridge around many academicians, it was important that I kept my children in the word. My kids were not easily influenced, even by me, so they asked lots of questions. They wanted to know things like, who wrote the Bible? Who compiled it together? If Adam and Eve were the first people, who did their kids marry? It's funny because these were the same questions that I myself had initially asked, and I studied so that I could answer their questions with as much clarity as I possibly could.

On the day that James gave his life to the Lord, it was just us there, and it was so beautiful. I wanted to call his dad and tell him, but I imagined that he was busy with a one-year-old and trying to juggle spending time with all the new lovers that he'd taken. Instead, I called my parents. They were happy because they'd raised him for the last year. My mom said, "I guess I did a good job with him." "You surely did, Mom," was my quick response. When I'm being fair and unbiased, I must give my ex-husband credit for doing a good job with our kids during their upbringing, especially my son. I had often wished that my ex-husband had hooked up with an older woman who would've been open to having his children around more, especially my son.

But because he chose to date so young, she couldn't possibly understand the need for a father to stay in his children's lives after he's no longer married to their mom. But throughout our lives, we did the best we could for them. I'd come to realize that people usually do the best that they can with what they have at the time. If he had more, he' would have given more. I was thankful that he always provided financially for them, though. I never had to ask nor beg for anything when it came to them. He set up bank accounts so that he could easily draft money to them, and all they had to do was text that they needed extra money for this or that. I had heard horror stories from other single moms about child support and finances. I decided during the divorce that I wouldn't ask for court-ordered child support and that we'd work that out on our own. It was a great decision on my part, and I thanked God that I didn't have to struggle financially with my children. I'd struggled already in other ways.

School was starting soon, and I started to look for a job. I had enough medical experience and two solid healthcare degrees yet learned very quickly that the south was a different ballgame when it came to salary and experience. I checked the newspapers daily for something within 30 miles of our house, but we only had one hospital in that radius. It was the same hospital that I was born in and though it had grown over the years, it was still decades behind some of the facilities that I'd worked for in Boston.

I took my time and looked for something, soon realizing that I'd likely be driving to Columbia or Charleston. I used all this free time to improve myself. Working on yourself can be hardest thing to do. We spend so much time worrying about other things that we hardly spend enough time in the mirror. We set crazy ideas in our minds about what's right or wrong and what's beautiful or ugly and it's all standards set by others.

When the kids were out at my mom's meeting their cousins, and playing at the park, I stayed in and spent time with God. I needed to flow like nature. I needed to teach others how to flow like nature, especially my family and friends. I began to practice and master the act of "non-judgement." This time in non-judgement meant that everything was the way it was because it was. I had to remind myself every time I'd start to judge something. For example, I thought that *the mosquitos are so bad in South Carolina* and corrected myself to *the mosquitos are a part of God's creation they are here just as I am.* To tell the truth, when I stopped focusing on their nuisance, their presence became less noticeable. After about two weeks, I could sit outside for hours at night and not get bitten by one single mosquito.

Finally, I got a job offer at a nuclear medicine practice in Columbia. It was a peaceful one-hour drive from the house. The kids started school the next week. The bus picked them up right in front of the house and dropped them off. I picked them up in the afternoon after basketball practice and any other after school activities. The job wasn't bad and the drive wasn't the best and so I used that hour each way to meditate and pray. I started practicing "speaking life." I understood that God has given me this power according to the word of God. How foolish was I not to have used it before?

I met the most beautiful woman at work. She was Spanish, and though she had children my age, her face was youthful. Her name was Miriam, and everyone called her Ms. T because her middle name was Travina, and she used her middle name instead of her first name. I fell instantly in love with Ms. T. She was an example of God's love. She made coming to work much easier for me because my salary was less than half of what I made in Boston. I know I had to understand the cost of living, and because I didn't have rent or mortgage, I was surely doing okay by southern standards. Ms. T and I talked about God every chance that we had.

I told her about my vision for changing the people in South Carolina. When you get a vision, you must be careful not to share it with everyone because some people will shoot it down, speak negatively against it, and discourage you. But Ms. T encouraged me all the way. In the first few months, it felt as though I'd known her my entire life. I left work empowered each day as I began my quest to change the worlds starting with my own community.

I started my first fitness/wellness group in South Carolina. Thank God for Ms. T's encouragement because it was hard to convince the people in South Carolina how bad sodas and McDonald's foods are for them and how important physical activity is for them. The group started with just a few of us, and then I watched it grow into a large group of women and men who had decided that they wanted to live healthy. I had to leave work and pick up the kids and be ready for my group meeting at seven. I got up at four o'clock to cook dinner each day and put it in the fridge before leaving for work. When we got home in the evening, all I had to do was warm it up and eat. We never missed eating dinner together unless there was an away game. The girls were playing volleyball, and my son was getting ready for the basketball pre-season to start. He'd be playing varsity again this year as a sophomore. Life was good these days, and things were flowing nicely like the Charles River.

On days that I missed Boston; I just imagined all the days shoveling my car out of four feet of snow. The weather in South Carolina was the best. Things were a tad bit slow, but I was really getting used to the change. And my kids were happy, genuinely happy. I tried to make them happy, but I understood that it's impossible to make anyone else happy when I'm not. The girls were getting used to the school, and though they missed their old friends, they had met some amazing new ones.

I couldn't wait to get to work in the morning to talk to Ms. T. I told her about my life and wanted to be totally truthful with her about my past. She carried this pureness about her that made me feel as if I was at the river in Cambridge—and she was never judgmental. I watched her eyes when I told her things that I'd been too embarrassed to tell own mom, and she didn't flinch. Her only reply was always, "Geneva, God loves you soooooooooo much." I once thought that Ms. T was an angel because she seemed to always have this glow of light radiating off her. Very soon I would learn that God had placed angels all around me, so that I would survive that *one thing* because it was now near.

10

Self-Love

Because I was starting to believe that God loved me so much, I asked myself, *How much do I love myself?* It was a hard question and an answer did not come quickly. *When you love someone, what's the first thing that you do?* I thought. *You tell them* was my speedy response. I realized that Tuesday morning on my way to work that in all the 37 years of my life I'd never told myself. I mean, I'd never looked at myself in the mirror and said those three words: *I love you.*

I immediately pulled the car over because I felt the need to do so boiling deep within me. Geneva needs to hear you say it; she needs you to look her in the eyes and tell her. I'd searched for love my entire life and little did I know the second greatest love next to God's love would come from myself.

When I pulled over to the dirt median part of the highway, I got a little nervous about it. I needed to do it, but I quickly became afraid to do it. *What if I did it the same way the others who said that they loved me had done it? What if I made this verbal declaration to this beautiful woman staring back into the rear-view mirror with eyes filled with tears? What if I didn't love her enough to wait for God to send her a good man, and instead I picked up again with someone who only wanted to share nightly pleasures with me?*

But Geneva needed me to love her. I cried and looked her in the eyes, this time not nervously looking away as I'd done for the last 10 minutes. This time, I looked deep within her, and I spoke the words repeatedly. *Geneva, I love you; Geneva Wallace, I love you; Geneva Wallace Grant, I love you; Geneva, I love you.* I accepted this love on that day. I accepted the fact that no one other than God could love me the way that I do. My mother had taught me this self-love, but as I ventured out into the world with the desire to be perfect, I lost all my self-love to short-term gratification. I had lost all my self-love trying to impress my neighbors, my colleagues, my family, and my friends.

Thank God I always left for work early because I looked down at the clock and noticed that I'd been sitting on the side of the road for the past hour. I got myself together and pulled out. I couldn't believe that for the past hour I had sat there on the side of the highway and told myself that I loved myself. It was the first time that I looked myself in the eyes and confessed my love.

I got to work just in time, and Ms. T could tell that I had revelation. I couldn't wait to tell her about it, but I first went through my emails and checked my voicemail. I walked over to her desk, and she said, "Geneva, you look like you're glowing this morning like you've found a new love." I told her all about the experience, and she just listened in awe. She said this was the beginning of the healing process and that God was about to use me in ways that I could never imagine. I felt rejuvenated. I wanted to dance. I wanted to sing. I wanted to cry more tears of joy. I went back to my desk and continued to work.

I was having the hardest time getting back to the school to pick up the kids after practices. Traffic in Columbia was hectic even though I left before the five o'clock rush hour. But God forbid it rained or there was an accident. Then it could take me hours to get home, which meant the kids would have to wait or my dad would have to go out of his way to pick them up. I really appreciated my dad for always dropping what he was doing to fill in for me. I was grateful that he'd been there for my only son for the last year, filling in all fatherly duties without hesitations.

I don't know how he did it with all the practices this boy had, and the drive seemed so long. I needed to find a job closer to home and closer to their school. I continued to look, but our small town didn't have much to offer.

Then I noticed a small privately owned family medical practice with an urgent care. I could see the growth potential in a place like that because it provided the only option to the town's Emergency Room, and their motto, "We will see you today," meant that they were equipped to handle a big schedule.

I applied and landed a job with the practice. It was owned and managed by a local family doctor with a heart of gold. He employed and later partnered seven other physicians, and all of them were compassionate, smart, innovative, and some of the most caring practitioner that I'd ever met. I would miss working with Ms. T, but we made a vow to keep in touch. She was happy for me because she knew how important being close to the kids meant to me.

Just two months into my new job, things were going great. Working so close to home and the kids' school had eased a lot of tension. I had more time to work on my wellness program, and the participants were all losing weight and feeling great. I got a few of my new co-workers to join me. I always told them it didn't make any sense that we worked with some of the best doctors in the south and we were not healthy. We have access to inside tips to staying healthy and living longer. And that was one amazing things about the physicians at Complete Care, they would always make time for the staff and their family members if they needed any kind of medical advice.

Life was great. I started to tell Geneva that I loved her every single day. And not only did I tell her, I showed her. Once a week, I stopped by the local neighborhood market and picked up fresh flowers for myself. I loved the smell of fresh flowers. I planted a rose bush for myself right next to the front porch. I started to write love poems again. I wrote some of my most beautiful writings during the next few weeks. When I had to wait for the kids to come to the car after practice, I wrote. We had our weekly Bible studies at home, and they were always filled with new lessons about God and life.

My son got his driver's permit right before we moved back and was not bugging me to take him to get his driver's license. I hated the idea of any of them driving. These rural roads were dark, and there were lots of deer. That seemed to be all he talked about lately. "Mom, it will save you some time, and I can pick up my sisters, too." It sounded good, but he was only 15. I didn't even realize that 15-year-old kids could drive in South Carolina.

I started to let him drive me around, and it felt good to be chauffeured. When I picked him up, I'd move over to the passenger side while I waited for him. I got a call from Ms. T one day, and I told her about his desire to drive. She said that her son was the same way and its normal. She said, "Teach him safety first and spend lots of time with him driving with you." And that's exactly what I did. I signed him up for the Driver's Ed class, which was mandatory. I also lectured him on the importance of safety while driving. I knew one day soon I was going to let him drive because he had proven himself repeatedly.

My oldest daughter said that she didn't want to learn to drive in South Carolina. She said that the roads were too dark. I agreed with her on that one, but "You'll have to learn to drive to get around without any public transportation." She replied, "When James gets his license, we will all just ride with him."

I remember that my sister had been the first to get her license. I wanted to drive but not as badly as she did. My dad took me everywhere I needed to go back them, which was usually just some kind of practice. I wasn't as anxious to drive as my son was now, but I scheduled to take him for his driver's test in a few weeks. I told him that we'd start shopping for a car at the beginning of next year. He got his driver's license and became the chauffeur for my mom, too. My mom never really enjoyed driving, so she now had James to drive her the 20 miles to the supermarket and to run errands on the Saturday mornings when he wasn't playing basketball.

My best friend Monique from high school had just moved back to South Carolina after relocating to Virginia for college over 15 years ago. It was nice to reconnect with her. She was beautiful and curvaceous. I always admired her and the way she dressed. I always tried to downplay or get rid of my curves, but she made me look at those curves as a blessing.

On days when she and I planned to meet for dinner, I had Monique pick me up, and I let the kids take the car to the mall or to the YMCA. It appears Monique and I had never been apart. I was always very proud of her. She had been raised by a strong mother who was a single parent and vowed that Monique would not be a statistic. She had gone off to college right after high school and always kept in touch. She worked for a real estate company in Virginia and seemed to have done well for herself. She was loving and genuine with a heart of gold. She had returned home to be closer to her mom, as I had done. She was single, so didn't have all of life's demands that I had, but she was still my friend. I loved spending time with her, and at first, I didn't tell her the details of my divorce, but I knew that I could. I never told her about the tragic day that I'd tried to end my life. She told me once over dinner she was proud of me. For the first time in a long time, I accepted it. I accepted that after all I'd been through, someone could still be proud of me. I have persevered through some dark nights, and though Monique didn't know all the details, she knew that I was a survivor of some things.

I was enjoying South Carolina more that I'd imagined. Things were slow, but the peace was surreal. I found a lake not too far from my house, and though it could not compare to the Charles River in Cambridge, it would suffice. I drove there after work and just spent time with God. I loved being alone in the presence of God. I prayed over my children's lives and practiced a technique that Ms. T had taught me to transfer positive energy and light to those I loved. I did so to the kids when I was down at the lake. Once my youngest daughter noticed, "Mom, when I was at practice today, I felt a warm feeling of love and light overcome me for a few minutes; it was weird." I told her that I had sent it to them through my thoughts. She replied, "Mom, that's too weird," but I sensed that she believed me.

We were just a few weeks away from Thanksgiving, and James had already began talking about basketball tournaments held in Myrtle Beach. Because I had just started a new job, I could not attend, but I looked forward to hearing about every play. Because he and I both shared a passion for the sport, we talk in great detail about defensive and offensive plays and why they worked or didn't work. This was going to be my first Thanksgiving with my parents and children in almost 18 years. I was so excited. Mom had even asked me to prepare potato salad and garden salad. I wasn't the greatest cook, especially when comparing myself to my family here in the south, but I'm so competitive that I just practiced for days on a special dish until I perfected it. I was in a great place and the air was so fresh here. It was so hard getting to sleep because I'd sit outside on the porch and never want to go inside. Even in November, the weather was beautiful. I envisioned shoveling out my car back in Cambridge and my heart smiled.

I could not contain my excitement about life. Just a year ago, I thought that I wouldn't make it and had almost given up on life. My wellness and fitness group was embarking on our first road race. I'd orchestrated a 5K event in my small hometown, the first of its kind, and was looking forward to a large turnout on this upcoming Saturday. During the days leading up to the race, things were very hectic but good. The kids were all playing sports, and though I had the luxury of working just a few miles from the school, it was still seven or eight o'clock by the time we got home on some evenings. I still had to meet with my wellness group, and the kids did a great job with getting dinner warmed up and the kitchen cleaned, so that by the time I was done, I could just shower and go to bed. Just a few days from my first road race, I laid in bed and thought that it had been months since I'd even thought about my ex-husband or any of the things in the past. It felt good to not be burdened with things that were out of my control. I thanked God that my life was moving forward, that I was no longer living a lie; instead, I was living my truth.

I set my alarm clock for four on the morning of the race. I needed to get up and get things done, so that I'd be ready to start the race at eight. I hired a race company out of Columbia, and they did everything pertaining to the race. I had to set up rest stops to give out water bottles and to encourage the runners and walkers. I was shocked to find the local newspaper there waiting to interview me about the event. They wanted to know what had made me want to do such an event in this small town. I wanted to respond, "Have you seen the federal statistics on health in South Carolina? We rank highest in the nation in high blood pressure, diabetes, and obesity." But instead I rephrased it nicely, took a few pictures, and got to work.

Hundreds of people showed up for the event, and the officers set up detours for the race. Vendors lined the streets, and we were ready to start. I met this very nice highway patrolman, Bobbie Phillips and his wife Carol, after I moved back earlier in the summer. He had experienced a near fatal car accident while responding to a call. When we first met, he told me about the experience and how he almost didn't make it. He said that the doctors didn't think he'd ever walk again, and here he was walking with a cane. I told him my plans for the race, and he told me that he'd be running the race with me. His beautiful petite wife smiled at the idea and shook her head like it would be impossible. I was so excited to see him on the day of the race getting registered. I was excited to see almost everyone in the town.

The town council had been very supportive of my ideas and didn't treat me like an outsider. I'd been away for a while, but we were still like family. Mrs. Francis Tomlin was one of my favorites, and she helped me the entire time by always asking me if there was anything else that she could do. We often walked together in the evenings, and I enjoyed our conversations. She was much older than me, and to the naked eye, we didn't have much in common, but our hearts connected. It was the same with another older couple, James and Annie Simms. They were very active in the community and were always ready and willing to help me. As a matter of fact, I received so much help with the event that it was almost weird. It was as if God had sent every single person and thing that I needed right to me, and relationships were forged that I'd cherish forever.

It was a beautiful day for a race, and as we gathered to pray, I felt the spirit of the Lord upon me. God was pleased because I was doing something great for his people. I was promoting good health and exercise and planting seeds in a community that would surely provide benefits for generations to come. My heart was humbled to tears. I cried silently as the gun fired and the race began. As we were nearing the end of the race, I saw Robbie and he was really pushing forward. I slowed down a bit until he caught up with me and we crossed the finish line together. Then we watched and cheered on the others behind us. The last person to finish the race had walked it in a little over an hour. My soul smiled when she said, "I've never walked this long in my life and I feel great."

This event made me think of the "Possum Trot," our town's only festival. A time when the small town got together in love. I had heard that racial tension still existed in the south, and I had felt it at times since I'd been back home, but today, we were a group of people from the same town with one common goal: "to improve our lives and the lives of those we love." God is love and, in this moment, I knew nothing else.

Thanksgiving was just a few days away. My family and friends were still talking about the event and wanted to know when was the next one. I vowed to do it annually, but spending Thanksgiving with my parents and children for the first time in so long was the only thing on my mind.

James had a Thanksgiving tournament in Myrtle Beach on the day before Thanksgiving, so I'd have to work the day before and pick him up later in the evening. Work was quiet as most people were preparing for the holiday. We met the morning before Thanksgiving for prayer in the staff lounge. This was one thing that I enjoyed most about my current job—they prayed together. We were a medical practice, and my physicians believed in God and not just medicine. I was honored to work for such amazing men.

I left early to head to the market to pick up my groceries for my meal. Then I went to the local lake and walked until dark. I needed to be out at the lake because I hadn't spent much private time with God because I'd been so busy the past few weeks, too busy to quiet down my mind and hear the voice of God. I walked for a very long time and was meditating on God's promise over my life when my phone rang. It was my son, and he wanted me to know that they had won the tournament and were headed back home. I could hear the excitement in his voice, and it made me happy. I had made many mistakes in life, but I'd always done the best I could with my kids and their happiness meant the most to me. I wanted them to look back on their childhood with joy. I promised him that I'd be there when he got home and that I couldn't wait to hear all the details of the games. They had played all day to win because it was a process of elimination: loser goes home, and winner moves on until the final game. He texted me a picture of him and his teammates holding their championship trophy, and I could feel his excitement.

I remembered the days in Boston when his AAU team was traveling and winning tournaments. We drove from city to city and watched them play. There was always a brotherhood on his basketball teams that he didn't have at home with two sisters. And his teammates were always more like brothers. I thought about all the times I'd entertained his teammates over dinner at our house or cookouts to celebrate wins.

11

That One Thing

———————⚜———————

I was waiting at the locked gate when the bus pulled up. I was not the first in line, as all the parents had gathered to pick their boys up along with the cheerleaders. As I watched James walking off the bus, I noticed how much taller and leaner he'd gotten. Had the boy grown in the past few days? He quickly hopped in the car and started reminiscing about the game, "Ma, there was this team from Columbia, had a center so tall, but Ma he wasn't that quick on his feet, so we put him in a box-and-one and shut him down." I listened as he explained the best players and games and talked about some of the awesome plays that he'd made. He then went on to say that all the boys were going to the movies to celebrate tonight and he wanted to go, too. "It's getting late, and I don't want you to drive alone. I'll ask your sisters if they want to come." He quickly replied, "Ma, we're taking our girlfriends and I've already asked Tonya to come with me."

My son had met Tonya during the last school year, and they started dating this summer. When the girls and I moved back, he told us that he wanted us to meet her right away. He said that she was pretty and shy but sweet. I'm thinking just some puppy love as she was older than him.

I remembered the summer day that I met her. We were campaigning for a local townsman who was running for an open Senate seat. He was running as the Republican for the vacant seat against a well-liked

Democrat. Tony Plummer was a smart and honest guy. I met him through a mutual friend, and after talking to him, he and I shared the same sentiments about the state of the people in our community, including our schools and ways that we could change things. I immediately jumped on his campaign during the election year that the first African American president was running for his second term as a Democrat and most people in the rural south were looking to vote straight Democrat without crossing party lines.

I had never been a fan of political parties, and I always took the time to examine candidates and what they could possibly bring to the future of my children. I asked James to come out with me on the campaign trail to go door to door in a heavily Democratic neighborhood. When I told him the location, his eyes lit up, "Ma, that's where Tonya lives. I want you to meet her." On the ride to her neighborhood, I told him that after we finished our door-to-door campaigning, we would go to her house. It was difficult to approach the homes of die-hard Democrats and explain to them why it's important to cross party lines during local elections. I told them about Tony's plan to help with the "educational crisis" in our district. As a mother, education is one of the most important topics when I'm considering local governmental candidates. Having my son with me, I also included that "this is about his future." And for me it was. The future of my son and two daughters was the most important thing in my life at that time.

We ended up at Tonya's right before evening. She lived in a small modest home with her parents and her aging grandmother. When we pulled up in the driveway, her parents were standing outside and they seemed overjoyed to see James.

Before we moved back to South Carolina, my dad had been bringing him here to see Tonya and waiting outside in the car. My dad was still the same, and he'd do anything for us. I never would've brought James all the way out here and waited in the car. Tonya lived outside of Rembert, which was not very close to our home here. James seemed excited for me to meet Tonya's family.

As I hopped out of the car, this beautiful young lady walked around the corner of the side of the house. She was dark and beautiful. She was petite and seemed very quiet. She kept her head down until she reached James, while avoiding eye contact with me. I didn't think anything was wrong with that as I'd been around shy people and she was shy. But I admired how beautiful she was. I could tell why my son had fallen hard for this older sweet girl. Her parents were just as nice and knew a lot about me. We stayed there for about an hour just chatting. This was refreshing. This was life, my new perfect life.

On the ride home James asked me what I thought of Tonya. "She's sweet and pretty, but you'll meet plenty of girls in your lifetime so don't get too serious." I'll never forget his reply, "Tonya will be my first and only girlfriend."

We were almost home, and he was still begging to go to the movies. His sisters said that they didn't feel like going, so "no" was the final answer. "But Ma, we're going to celebrate our win tonight, and you know I'm always safe in the car, and I'll be right back after the movie." The answer was still "no," but then he did something that softened my heart and something that he hadn't done in years. He moved in closely to me and grabbed my hand, "Ma, please let me go. I'll pick Tonya up and meet the team at the movies and drop her home and come right back." I used to love holding his hand when he was a little boy. It was something special about the relationship between mother and son in the same sense that it had been between my father and me. I turned into pudding and replied, "Yes, you can, but you have to promise to obey all of the driving rules and come right back after the movies."

My oldest daughter jumped up and said that she didn't think that it was a good idea because Tonya didn't live close. Ariel jumped in and said that "James always gets his way." I didn't believe that to be the truth, but he had proven himself all summer to be a good and responsible driver. For a fact, I trusted him to drive his sisters to the movies and the mall all the time.

I noticed that I left all my bags in the trunk of the car. I told my son to go grab them and then he could go to the movies. I had planned to peel the potatoes for the salad tomorrow, but after James left, I didn't feel like doing much. The girls had gone to their rooms and seemed to be bothered by the fact that I'd just let James sweet talk me into a night out with his friends.

I laid down, but my mind wouldn't quiet down. I dozed off. I'm on the Charles River in Cambridge not too far from my old house in Harvard Square. There's snow on the ground, but there's no ice on the river. In fact, the river looks like a summer day, but it's cold. I'm wearing my favorite North Face jacket and it's keeping me warm, but I'm wearing flip-flops. A deer passes by running fast as if in danger. That's weird. I've never seen deer in Cambridge. The sky is a floral pink, and the sun is shining bright, and the snow is almost three feet high. This seems all wrong. I'm confused.

Someone's calling my name, not my entire name, but my last name. "Ms. Wallace." "What's going on?" I jumped up, startled. It was a dream, but someone's knocking on the back door. "Oh, my God, it's James. Thank God, he's back. I was worried to death. Where's your key, James? Why are you knocking so hard on the door?"

As soon as I opened the door, a man stepped in. "Why are you stepping into my home? What time is it? Where's James? Why is there a police officer with you? I'm lost. I'm confused. My words have come to life. Death has come for my husband's child." I heard the man say, "I'm Coroner Baker."

"This cannot be true." I collapsed to the floor, and the next thing I remember is being in the arms of my mother. She's cradling and rocking me. My dad is sitting next to us, and he looks as if a train has hit him. "Where are Ariel and Naomi?"

"Momma, what time is James coming home?" I'm so confused. I hear people all over my house. I do not see faces, but I hear voices: my sisters, my aunts, my cousins, my Godmother, my neighbors. I can't breathe or think with all these people here. "Isn't it Thanksgiving? It is Thanksgiving."

My mom said, "There was an accident, and we lost James, Geneva." This has got to be some joke or dream. I'm dreaming. "Daddy, please tell me I'm dreaming."

"Geneva you're not dreaming," he replied. My life is ending right now. I must die because there is no way that I can live without him.

"Can someone please take me to see him? My God, where are you? Please help me."

I woke up the next day, and Monique was standing near the end of the bed. "Geneva, we're going to have to plan a funeral. I will take care of the arrangements, just tell me what you want." Didn't she know that there was nothing that I wanted other than to have my only son here with me? I knew that Monique was my friend and when we said that we'd do anything for each other, I hadn't imagined in a million years that she'd have to help me bury any of my kids. She would prove herself to be an angel as she planned every detail as if she was me. She knew that I'd like this or that. She knew that simple was the best. For the next few days, I remember very little. My daughters laid with me for hours. My ex-husband came, and we all laid on the floor in his room, still smelling the sweat from his basketball uniform that he left at the foot of his bed.

One of the doctors from work came over to check on my health. I couldn't eat or sleep. He ordered a prescription, and my ex-husband picked it up from the pharmacy and made sure that I took it. Monique says that I must wear a black dress, and her baby sister Angela had picked one up for me. She had everything written down in a notebook with instructions, I guess, on how things would go. She came often to tell me something. "When will I get to see him?" Monique dropped her head and said, "I'll go get your mom, and she'll explain that to you." My mom came in and said, "Geneva, there was a car fire and there is no body." I felt my chest sinking in, all the oxygen leaving my lungs. I passed out.

I woke up to prayer. Somebody was praying for me. I knew her voice, though I couldn't see her face. Myeisha. She came here from Boston and was praying. I heard her calling on the Lord to help me and my family. But it angered me. Why are you praying? If God really cared anything about me, he'd never allow me to feel this kind of pain. I yelled out in pure outrage, "Everyone shut up! God is not here and will never be here! Don't you know that my only son is dead?" My mom and dad moved in quickly to take me back to my room. My mom said, "She's out of it with the medication." But I wasn't out of it, I knew what I was saying, and I meant what I had said. I can't remember much about the next few days. I know that my family and friends were always there. I was on a "suicide watch" because I mentioned dying and my parents knew that I'd attempted suicide before, so they had decided that someone would stay with me 24 hours a day. My ex-husband returned to Boston after two weeks, and he promised that he would return to help me and the girls make it through.

Weeks passed and I was so weak and fragile. So broken and torn. I'd rather be dead than to live with this heartache. Sure, I missed on the first attempt, but I knew that I could get my hands on a handgun and get this over with quickly.

One afternoon, my daughters were watching me sleep. I felt them both lying next to me and looking into my face. I'm sure I didn't resemble their mom because I hadn't eaten whole food in weeks, except the soup that they force-fed me. I rolled over to face the wall and the words left my mouth, "I don't want to live without James." The room fell silent, and Ariel who was usually the quietest of the two spoke loudly, "What about us, Mom? Naomi and I are still here. Did you know that we didn't die in the accident? Was James your only child?"

Another sharp pain hit my heart, and I was sure that I was having a heart attack. Naomi chimed in, "Mom, do you realize that when James went to the movies that night that was the first time that he went to the movies without us? Do you realize that all of us could've died in that car fire?"

I started to sob. I hadn't thought about that. I hadn't thought about them. I was the same selfish woman who had wanted so badly to keep an appearance of a perfect life that I wished death upon my husband's child out of wedlock. Now here I was suffering through the pain that I wished fell upon someone else.

On that day, my life changed. I accepted the words of my daughters as the truth, and for the first time in weeks, I opened my mouth to pray to God just to thank him that I had not lost all three of my children. I thanked God for Ariel and Naomi's lives. I wasn't sure how my life was going to be after this *one thing*. The accident surely changed my life forever, but I had to live because there were two beautiful young girls who needed me more than ever right now. They had been closer to their brother than I had been. It had always been the three of them playing together while I was cooking dinner. They had walked home from school together while I was working. They had stayed up all night waiting to open Christmas gifts, and they had spent days in the backyard playing in the snow and making snow angels. They had lost their best friend and brother and, in all my pain and grief, I had forgotten about them.

I needed God, and I needed him more than I could've imagine. I called for him on a Thursday morning and he answered. I asked him for a second chance and promised that I'd never speak death again. I'd spend the rest of my days speaking life. His reply is forever engraved on my heart, "Go out and heal the nation. Save the people with the truth and never get caught up in a lie or misperception. I am God and you are my servant. I will give you many sons and they will live forever as James will, too."

ABOUT THE AUTHOR

Tomeka Walker Ewing is a native of Pinewood, SC, having spent most of her adult years in Cambridge, Massachusetts. She recently returned home to South Carolina and currently resides in Charleston, SC. She is a Minister of the Gospel, a spoken word artist, a motivational speaker, and soon to be acclaimed author.

She is the mother of three beautiful children Khadijah, Stanley (who now resides in heaven with the Lord), and Asia Ewing. She is the eldest daughter of John Earl Walker Sr. and Joan Walker in whom she contributes all that she is and will be in this life.

She is a radical lover of God and of words. Tomeka has been a healthcare administrator for over 15 years, and when she's not working you can find her on the nearest beach spending quality time with God's perfect creation.